DESERT DEADEYE

When the range was right, he gently nudged the rifle's trigger. A thundering report ended the desert silence. The Winchester slammed into his shoulder, yellow flame spitting from its barrel as the explosion echoed across the brushlands surrounding the dry stream. The tracker jerked in his saddle, emitting a piercing scream when he was torn from the back of his plunging, rearing horse.

Slocum levered another shell, swinging his gun sights to a man aboard a pinto. With fractions of a second to get his aim, he squeezed off a second shot, wincing when the roar of his gun came so close to his right ear. A Mexican toppled from the pinto . . .

JAKE LOGAN

BLOOD ON THE RIO GRANDE

J

JOVE BOOKS, NEW YORK

BLOOD ON THE RIO GRANDE

A Jove Book / published by arrangement with
the author

PRINTING HISTORY
Jove edition / May 1996

The Putnam Berkley World Wide Web site address is
http://www.berkley.com

ISBN: 0-515-11860-5

A JOVE BOOK®
Jove Books are published by The Berkley Publishing Group,
200 Madison Avenue, New York, New York 10016.
JOVE and the "J" design are trademarks
belonging to Jove Publications, Inc.

PRINTED IN THE UNITED STATES OF AMERICA

10 9 8 7 6 5 4 3 2 1

BLOOD ON
THE RIO GRANDE

1

City Marshal Tom Spence surveyed the scene, scowling. Blood covered the ground inside low hacienda walls where Howard Anderson's *vaqueros* had put up a valiant fight to the last man. Tom knew simple *vaqueros* were no match for experienced *pistoleros* of the kind who rode with Victoriano Valdez. Valdez employed some of the best hired gunmen in northern Mexico to take part in his revolution; to attempt an overthrow of the government in Mexico City. What didn't make sense to Tom right then was why Valdez had crossed the Rio Grande to pull a raid in Texas. One obvious answer might lie in Howard's huge herd of blooded horses, good thoroughbred remount stock that would give Valdez mounted superiority when the Federales took up his trail across Tamaulipas and Coahuila. Mounted on better horses, he would be much harder to catch in the wilds of northern Mexico. But Tom knew Howard Anderson's missing daughter was of pressing importance. During the raid, Melissa had somehow fallen into the hands of Valdez and his gunmen.

Howard grieved as anyone should expect he might over the knowledge that his beautiful daughter was with a ruthless border cutthroat like Victoriano. He needed no help imagining what these lawless bandits would do to a pretty young girl like Melissa, a blond beauty who was the talk of Laredo society. Not only was she remarkably beautiful, but she was also rich. The Anderson ranch was one of the largest in Webb County: thousands of cattle and horses, business interests in the city of Laredo, and a fortune in real estate. Had Victoriano known this when he planned his raid and captured her? Several hundred head of Anderson's best horses were missing, yet Howard thought nothing of losing horses. It was his daughter he wanted back, and he was willing to pay handsomely for her return. A ten thousand dollar cash reward would be given to whoever brought Melissa out of Mexico unharmed. But who would risk going up against the paid *pistoleros* of Victoriano Valdez to make the rescue? Only a madman would attempt it—or someone who understood the rules of mortal combat when the odds were stacked heavily in another's favor.

Howard paced back and forth across the blood-soaked caliche with his hands clasped firmly behind his back. Tom saw the agony in his eyes when Howard paused to stare across the battleground that was his front yard. More than a dozen bodies lay in the sun, men who had given up their lives in defense of the Anderson ranch. It was a grisly scene that needed no words to describe it. Green-backed blowflies swarmed around the corpses, adding their buzzing noise to the grinding of Howard's boots as he marched from one body to the next, halting just long enough to identify the dead before he continued his purposeful walk inside the low adobe wall around his magnificent home.

"They all died bravely," Howard observed, casting a wavering glance around the yard. His voice sounded strained, like he was choking.

"You can see they put up one hell of a fight," Tom

agreed, for there was little else he could say.

Howard's eyes misted. "They gave up their lives to protect Melissa. All for nothing. Now Valdez has her, and only God knows where he will take her. I suppose I should be glad her mother is not alive to see this dark day . . ."

The buzzing flies droned endlessly. Tom was trying to think of a solution. "I'll notify the Federale commander over yonder in Nuevo Laredo, but you know as well as I do they won't be able to find Victoriano. I doubt they'll try very hard."

"Perhaps the reward will interest a few good bounty hunters who aren't afraid to cross the Rio Grande," Howard said quietly. "Ten thousand dollars is a lot of money."

Tom toed the ground with a boot. "It may not be enough to get the job done, Howard. Hell, you'd have to send an army down there. I've been told Valdez has close to a hundred followers."

Howard wasn't in the mood for bad news. "Goddamn it, Tom, I want my daughter back! Don't tell me it can't be done!"

"I was only saying . . ." Tom's voice trailed off. It served no purpose to dash the poor man's hopes. "We all understand how you feel." He noticed buzzards circling lower in the skies above the ranch, drawn by blood smell. A boy riding a burro had been sent for the undertaker. It would take all day to remove so many bodies from Howard's yard. Watching the chore would only worsen his grief. He had no wife to console him—Melissa's mother died giving birth to her. "Why don't you ride back to town with me? No sense hangin' around until the undertaker shows up. Nothing much you can do here."

"I'll stay," Howard replied tonelessly. He gave Tom a look. "Make sure you send those wires advertising the reward money. If anyone inquires, I want to talk to them personally.''

Tom merely nodded while turning for his horse. In his heart he knew no one would ever earn the reward. Rescuing Melissa from the clutches of Victoriano Valdez was downright impossible in the wilds of Mexico. Troops of Federales had been hounding him for years without result. Valdez was smart, too smart to let himself get boxed in by a superior force. It would take brains, not big armies, to track him down and take the girl. The men who undertook such a task would need nerves of steel and more cunning than a fox.

As Tom mounted his bay, an old memory awakened in the back of his mind, a recollection of a man he'd known during the war. If John Slocum were pitted against Valdez, it would make an interesting contest. Slocum had plenty of nerve, and enough raw courage for two men. Perhaps more than anything else, he'd known when to fight and when to run. Almost instinctively, Slocum had shown a keen understanding of the enemy. And when it came time to fight, he became a deadly adversary with a knowledge of weapons beyond the average soldier. With guns or knives or fists, John Slocum met few men who were his equal. The last Tom heard of him he was in Denver working as a railroad detective.

''I knew this feller once,'' Tom began thoughtfully. ''Back durin' the war. Last I heard, he was a detective up in Denver. His name's John Slocum an' he might have some ideas on how to get Melissa back. I'll send a wire up there in care of the city marshal's office. If Slocum's still around Denver, maybe the marshal can get word to him.''

Howard gave Tom a disinterested look. ''I doubt a detective will do any good. Bounty hunters is what I need; men who aren't afraid of a fight.''

Tom chuckled softly. "If there's one thing Slocum ain't afraid of, it's a scuffle. Difference is, Slocum knows when to fight."

"But he's just one man, Tom. Surely you can see that one man won't be enough."

"Kinda depends on the man, Howard. Slocum's smart. Maybe a little on the crazy side, too. He ain't afraid of nothin', even when he oughta be. I'll send that telegram. Won't hurt to see if he's interested in makin' a big payday."

"It's probably a waste of time. Besides, Denver is too far away for him to get here quickly enough. Valdez will stay on the move, making it harder and harder to track him down as the days go by. I want those notices posted everywhere, Tom. I need men, good men with guns, and I need them in a hurry."

Tom lifted his reins to ride off. "I'll spread the word as far as I can." He gazed across the blood-soaked compound again, then to the sky where black vultures circled. "Sorry this had to happen," he added gently. "Nobody believed Valdez would be so bold as to strike north of the Rio Grande. I figure it was them good horses of yours he wanted. Melissa just happened to be in the wrong spot at the wrong time."

Howard's features became frozen. He watched the horizon to the south, toward Mexico. "They'll hurt her, Tom. Even if I can get her back, she'll never be the same. Men like that will have no mercy in them. They'll use her in the most awful ways. She's only a girl, too young to understand men like Valdez and his paid guns . . . how they treat their women. Dear God! I just can't bring myself to think about what she must be going through and yet I must face the truth. She'll be their whore . . . until they have no more use for her."

Tom wasn't quite sure what to say. "Because she's so

pretty they're more likely to keep her alive. No need to explain why, I don't reckon.''

Howard nodded that he understood. ''The cruelty of it is so obvious, taking a girl so young, forcing her to do things against her will. I doubt I'll be able to sleep thinking about it, about what she's going through.''

''Nothin' I can say will make any difference. You know as well as me what they'll do to her. Main thing is to get her back if we can. I'll post those notices an' send that wire to Denver. If I can find John Slocum, he'll have some pretty good ideas what to do if there's time. Time's our biggest enemy right now.'' Tom swung his horse away from the adobe wall. ''Be seein' you, Howard. If you need anything, let me know. I'll keep you posted.'' He roweled his bay to a jog trot away from the ranch, wishing there was more he could do to lessen Howard's pain.

On the ride back to Laredo, Tom Spence thought of John Slocum. It had been years since the war ended. Tom remembered that Slocum planned to go home to Georgia after Lee surrendered. Like everyone else, he meant to start a new life as soon as the killing stopped. But then Tom had heard that Slocum was in the West again—in Denver—last he heard. Slocum was an imposing figure, just over six feet and hard as iron, with black hair and the coldest green eyes Tom had ever seen. His movements were sure, practiced, spare. Born in a small town in Georgia, to a farming family, it was hardly the sort of beginning anyone expected for a man who became so proficient at fighting. Killing. Slocum had a knack for applying just the right amount of force and knowing when to use it. Tom found himself hoping he could locate Slocum before it was too late.

He rode into Laredo, down dusty streets, lost in thought until he came to his tiny office between storefronts on the main caliche road running down to the river crossing into

Mexico. Just once, as he swung down from the saddle, he took a look across the Rio Grande at Nuevo Laredo. No one would argue that Mexico was a world apart from Texas when it came to law and order. Below that river, the law of the gun ruled more often than not. Stronger men took what they wanted by using guns, and there was little anyone could do about it. Men like Victoriano Valdez became mightier when they banded together to form gangs. Valdez understood this all too well. The size of his revolutionary force made him even more formidable.

Tom tied his horse and climbed a sagging wooden boardwalk to his office door, thinking about how he would word offers of the reward from Howard Anderson. If Tom was any judge of hard men, it wouldn't be long before Laredo was crawling with unscrupulous types seeking the money. Bounty hunters and back-shooters were sure to show up in large numbers when word of a ten thousand dollar reward spread, making it even more difficult to enforce city ordinances and keep the peace. Laredo was a tough town in the first place, a jumping-off place for men on the run from the law headed into Mexico. Now things would only get worse.

He unlocked his office door and entered a sweltering room with a row of cagelike cells at the back. For now, the cells were empty; however, that was a condition Tom was sure would change once word got out of Howard Anderson's reward money.

Tom sank into a chair behind his desk and took a breath of stale air. Then he reached for a fountain pen and an inkwell to prepare notices about the reward. On a separate piece of foolscap, he worded another message, to the city marshal of Denver, inquiring as to the whereabouts of John Slocum.

After the telegrams were written, Tom got up to make for the telegraph office, wondering if he were about to unleash forces that might worsen the bloodbath in Webb County. He was powerless to prevent Howard from offering so much money for his daughter's safe return, but down in his gut, Tom knew the reward would touch off another round of bloodletting and killing. There was something about the combination of money and guns that always brought about a goodly measure of trouble.

2

A slender blond girl, only three weeks from her eighteenth birthday, lay atop a four-poster bed, her wrists and ankles tied to the bedposts. In pale lamplight, the bearded man towering over her brandishing a long Bowie knife seemed demonic, an evil thing, his face twisted into a network of deep lines etched in a leathery mask of skin the color of creamed coffee. A black beard clung to his cheeks and chin in twists and curls that were matted in tight little knots. When he grinned cruelly, a gold tooth at the front of his mouth caught and reflected the glow from a lantern on a table beside the bed. Melissa Anderson lay stunned, barely able to move, spread-eagled on a stained, foul-smelling mattress.

Victoriano Valdez undressed her with his obsidian eyes as his gaze moved along her body, pausing at her breasts, then on the cleft of her thighs. Her blue gingham dress had been torn during their flight deep into Mexico. And now, as Victoriano stared at the buttons down the front of her thin summer gown, she opened her mouth to scream, for she knew he meant to cut her clothes off and use her body.

''Be silent, yellow-haired bitch!'' he growled in Spanish, ''or I will hit you again.'' He had delivered a sharp blow to her face just moments earlier when she cried out while her hands and feet were being tied to the bed. Blood trickled from one corner of her mouth, running down her porcelain cheek to a pillow below her head.

Victoriano looked over his shoulder. A *pistolero* with two bandoliers crisscrossing his chest stood near the door with a rifle. ''Leave us alone, Juanito,'' Victoriano commanded. ''Shoot anyone who comes near the adobe. Tell Alvaro to make sure the men have plenty of tequila while I teach this gringo bitch how to make love to a man.''

''*Si, jefe*,'' Juanito said, opening a thin plank door for a look outside. He grinned when he cast a backward glance at the girl. ''She is a beautiful woman, the most beautiful woman I have ever seen. Perhaps she is a virgin? If I hear her screaming, I will know—''

''Get out!'' Victoriano snapped, returning his attention to the girl. He lowered the tip of his knife to the top button on her dress and sliced it off. When the button fell, he laughed and cut off another button, then one more, until the front of her dress fell open, revealing a lace bodice gathered at the front by a cotton cord. He sliced the cord in half, the tip of his knife making a tearing sound. The girl gasped, eyes rounding with fear when Victoriano bent over her to cup one small, firm breast in a callused hand.

''Do not scream!'' he shouted in thickly accented English. ''Or I will cut your throat. Be silent if you wish to live to see the sun rise again.'' He placed the tip of his knife to her neck so it pricked her skin, drawing a trace of blood. Then he squeezed her breast, pinching her nipple between his thumb and forefinger. Melissa squirmed, but she made no sound, even when he increased pressure around her rosy pink nipple while the knife was held to her windpipe. Tears flooded her eyes. Her arms and legs trembled. Her tongue flicked out to catch some of the blood running from her lips, and when Victoriano saw this, he laughed. "Stupid *puta!*" he cried. "You are nothing but a white man's whore! Damn you! Stop your whimpering!"

Melissa closed her eyes. Everything seemed unreal. She wished it was just a bad dream, and soon she would wake. The attack on the ranch was now only a blur. It had happened too quickly. Her father's loyal *vaqueros* had died in a hail of bullets, trying to defend the house. Then the door to her bedroom was battered down by four gun-wielding bandits who dragged her downstairs. Waiting for her was the leader of the gang whom the others called Victoriano, a loathsome giant with an oily, unwashed smell. As he bent over her now, his breath reeking of liquor, Melissa understood what he was about to do to her. He intended to have his way with her and if she fought him, he might kill her.

She felt him knead her breast roughly, causing more pain, although she could not open her eyes. A series of tremors raced down her arms and legs. She flinched when something touched the top of her underwear, the cold steel of Victoriano's knife. A ripping sound startled her when her undergarment was torn from her hips. She lay naked, stretched out on the bed, her mound and breasts exposed, tattered remnants of her dress lying around her. The moment was at hand and she knew this, even though she had never before been with a man.

Victoriano grunted, and through slitted eyelids Melissa saw him unfasten his pants. As he pulled them off his hips, his cock stood erect, pulsing with blood. Melissa had never seen a prick so large. A few times she'd witnessed a vaquero urinating behind the barn when she came around a corner too quietly. But in all her life she had never seen a cock so thick or so long, blunted at the head, much too large to enter her without causing terrible agony or tearing her tender flesh.

The bed shook when Victoriano came between her parted thighs and his foul smell threatened to overwhelm her. She drew back against the mattress as far as she could and held her breath for the moment when he thrust himself inside her. She caught a brief glimpse of the knife in his hand. He squeezed her right breast harder until it was all she could do to stifle a cry by pressing her lips together.

"Lie very still, *mi hita*," he warned, lowering his body over hers. His tremendous weight almost crushed her and she feared she would not be able to breathe.

A soft whimper escaped her mouth despite her best efforts to silence it. She felt the head of his cock touch the hair of her mound. She was surprised to find herself wet, the way she got at night when she allowed herself to dream about what making love to a man would be like. It infuriated her that she would get wet at a time like this, with a man so repulsive, so revolting. Why was she so aroused by being taken against her will?

His powerful hand crushed her breast, squeezing her flesh in a viselike grip. It was all she could do to keep from screaming as a fresh wave of tears filled her eyes. But the most excruciating pain she had ever known followed immediately thereafter, as the head of Victoriano's cock pushed the lips of her cunt apart. Melissa gasped, eyes bulging wide. "No!" she cried, wagging her head back and forth atop the pillow. "Please . . . don't do this to me!"

He answered her with a cruel laugh, shoving his prick deeper inside her. Pain radiated from her mound like chains of lightning in a thunderstorm, crackling with intensity. Her abdomen shook violently, her thighs quivering while she tried desperately to pull away from his rock-hard member. It felt as if something was being torn inside her.

"It will feel good," he whispered hoarsely, his lips close to her ear. "Tonight you will become a woman."

Again, he thrust himself deeper into her cunt, and when she felt the girth of his prick, she screamed at the top of her lungs until it seemed the rafters above the bed trembled. Before her scream died in her throat he struck her with an open palm, and the force of the blow sent her mind reeling. Winking stars appeared before her eyes— she tasted fresh blood and her left cheek ached with a thousand bee stings. She struggled against her restraints uselessly, hoping to free her arms. Another cry came involuntarily from deep in her chest, a cry of pain and humiliation she could not suppress.

"Shut up, bitch!" Victoriano snarled, leering down at her. He thrust his hips downward, sending another inch of cock into her moist cunt. Renewed pain in her groin made her forget about the vicious blow to her face. Her head lolled to one side and she lay still in a state of shock while more of his prick was pushed inside her. It felt like a tree trunk was wedged between the lips of her mound. The girth of his shaft made her feel as if she would explode or split in two halves. She fought back more tears— this filthy bandit was taking her virginity and she would never be the same again. No decent man would ever want her for a wife after tonight. Her life would be ruined.

Only seconds later, he began to thrust back and forth, in and out of her in a short, jerky motion. Melissa could hear the wet juices in her cunt making a sucking noise when he pulled back for another deep thrust into her womb. She wanted to scream each time his length penetrated her, yet she knew it would only anger him, and he would hit her again. It was utterly useless to resist.

Victoriano began to pant with exertion. Sweat beaded

on his face and neck, his chest. The bed squeaked each time he rocked forward, and his terrible smell increased the odor of sweat and tequila. He placed his knife on the pillow beside her head in order to grab a fistful of her hair. Thrusting, panting, he made each penetration harder, more forceful, until the full weight of his groin hammered against her stomach.

"Please," she whimpered softly, "don't hurt me."

His breath came in ragged bursts now, and his thrusts quickened. The wet sound in her cunt grew louder, as his cock sucked her juices out when his shaft withdrew. And as the tempo of his thrusting increased, a strange new sensation hinting of pleasure started in Melissa's womb. She resisted it with all her might, embarrassed by it. Why would it feel good to have a man take her by force? It wasn't possible, and yet a warm feeling had begun inside her . . . or was she only imagining it?

Victoriano grunted each time his cock slammed into her cunt. He was sweating profusely, trembling with desire, and noises made by the squeaking bed were louder, more distinct.

"Please don't hurt me," Melissa groaned, enveloped by a new feeling, a bewildering combination of pleasure and pain.

The rhythm of his thrusts became faster. Wet sucking sounds accompanied each movement he made, and he gasped for air. Along with the increase in his heavy breathing, his hips gyrated downward more forcefully. Soon, Melissa's cunt felt like it was on fire with sensations she never knew she had. In a way she could not explain, it felt as if she were about to explode. She was not thinking about Victoriano's smell or his sweat trickling down onto her naked body. Something about the experience had changed and it was not altogether unpleasant.

She found herself meeting his thrusts with her own, before she realized what she was doing. Some frenetic energy had taken over her actions, and now they were beyond her control. Arching her spine, she drove her mound against his shaft with a rhythm equal to his and while she did this, more of the warm tingling spread through her cunt.

"You like it, gringo bitch!" Victoriano said.

Had she been able, she would have denied it, yet for now the pleasure almost outweighed the pain, and she found she was unable to speak.

"Tell me you like it!" he shouted, drawing his lips back over his teeth, a demand Melissa didn't fully comprehend in the throes of his passion.

"No!" she hissed, unwilling to give in to him at a time like this, forced against her will to do his bidding.

His fist knotted more deeply into her golden hair. He gave a jerk with his hand, awakening her to a new form of pain.

"Tell me you like it!" he cried again.

It did seem her pleasure heightened somewhat, but she would rather have died than admit this to him now. "No," she whimpered quietly, protesting as much as she dared.

He slapped her, harder than before, and she almost lost consciousness. Her mouth filled with blood and she noticed a cut on her lower lip after she ran her tongue across it. When she tried to speak, the words came out garbled, indistinct.

Then a sudden burst of sensation overtook her, the warmth of something deep within her groin gaining intensity. Her pelvis rocked against Victoriano's cock frantically in spite of the hurt and embarrassment she felt. Straining every muscle in her body, her limbs turned to iron. She trembled and let out a cry that was animal-like, not of her own making. Her womb convulsed. As the sensation grew, she let herself go, no longer fighting it as she had before.

Victoriano shuddered. A flood of warm wetness spilled from his testicles. Pumping, grunting, gasping for air, he sent his seed into her belly in a series of mighty thrusts. He groaned as his jism flowed and for a moment he went rigid, straining, a look of ecstasy on his face. Seconds later he collapsed on top of her, completely spent.

Melissa found she was unable to breathe with his heavy body on top of hers. He was crushing her, and yet there was something about the experience that was curiously enjoyable.

"You . . . are . . . too . . . heavy," she gasped, squirming underneath him.

He did not seem to hear her.

"Please get off . . . of me," she begged, turning to one side so his weight was less oppressive.

Victoriano's eyes batted open. He stared down at her for a time while still breathing hard, drops of sweat dripping off his cheeks and a few tiny hairs at the end of his beard.

She felt his cock soften inside her, and that was when the realization struck her that she was no longer truly whole. She had given up her virginity at knifepoint to a Mexican bandit and the thought of what she had done left her feeling empty, alone. It wasn't that she'd had a choice, for she was certain that her life hung in the balance. But now, as the moment passed, she began to experience deepening sorrow.

She gazed up at the ceiling. At least she was alive, and if the opportunity came, she might be able to escape the clutches of Victoriano and get back to her father's ranch in Texas. She told herself that patience was necessary, awaiting the right opportunity. Until then, she must do whatever it took to stay alive.

3

Slocum propped his boots on the iron veranda railing and lit a rum-soaked cheroot. He tasted sweet smoke and gave a contented sigh before picking up his brandy snifter. Good brandy was hard to find in San Antonio; only the best places, such as the Saint Anthony Hotel, offered quality liquors and fine cigars. It was one reason he hired a room here whenever he was in San Antone on business—or pleasure. Glancing over his shoulder past the French doors into his suite, he briefly considered an abundance of pleasure he'd found on this trip. Pleasure came in the form of a woman last night, as his pleasures so often did. Belle was quite a woman. He saw her sleeping below a lace canopy above the bed and the sight brought him sweet recollections of the previous evening. Her soft, passionate body had been just what he needed after a long train ride in blistering summer heat from Fort Worth to San Antonio. As a crimson sunrise greeted him this morning, he thought about the telegram in his coat pocket and the reason he had come to south Texas.

A wire from an old friend he hadn't seen since the war had abruptly ended his stay in Fort Worth. Tom Spence had gone to a considerable amount of trouble tracking him down. And the mention of a ten-thousand-dollar reward was no small matter. If Tom said there was ten thousand dollars to be made for locating a captive teenage girl in Mexico, it was information Slocum trusted. He and Tom had served together in the Army of Virginia during the worst years of the war and they knew each other well, having fought side by side at Bull Run and later as a part of Pickett's charge under the command of Stonewall Jackson. Sharing that brutal war experience made Slocum and Tom fast friends, even now, after all the years that had passed.

Slocum wondered about the girl in Mexico. According to the wire, she had been captured by a gang of border outlaws during a raid across the Rio Grande in Texas. Slocum knew little about all the troubles going on in Mexico beyond reports he'd read in the newspapers. Another revolution was brewing down there and all manner of men from the states were hiring out as mercenaries to help bring down what was widely reported to be a corrupt government in Mexico City. But these revolutionary bands were said to be a mix of lawless pirates and dedicated patriots. It was hard to tell one bunch from another, so the stories went. But for a princely sum like ten thousand dollars, Slocum knew he was willing to take a few calculated risks in order to find out if the girl could be freed. Making discreet inquiries seldom got too dangerous if a man knew what he was about and watched his back.

He took a puff from his cheroot and let the smoke lift in lazy swirls on a breath of warm morning wind. He'd be boarding a train for Laredo before noon and by tomorrow he would know more about the girl's abduction. Only then would he decide if there were a chance to successfully arrange for the release of Melissa Anderson. Until then he would think about the ten thousand and how he could spend it, a nice way to pass a few morning hours.

A soft knock on the door announced the arrival of their food, and he got up to let the waiter in. Having breakfast sent up to his room was something he regularly did while staying at the Saint Anthony, in part because of the wonderful view his room had of the city and the San Antonio River. Granted, it was a luxury he rarely could afford, but this stay in San Antone was a special treat for himself.

As a precaution, he touched the butt of a small belly-gun he carried inside his shirt before opening the door. The little .32 caliber Colt had saved his life a number of times. Being careful was so much a part of his nature that he rarely gave any thought to it. While he usually relied on a .44-.40 Peacemaker revolver when trouble came his way, he still carried the belly-gun on most occasions. At close quarters, the .32 was deadly if a man could hit what he was aiming at with a short-barreled pistol.

He opened the door a crack and saw a waiter balancing a tray. The aroma of fresh coffee and the scent of fried bacon made Slocum's mouth water. "Bring it in," he said quietly. "Try not to disturb the lady sleeping in the next room."

There was something about Slocum's admonition that gave the young Mexican waiter pause, but after a moment of hesitation he came in and set the tray down on a polished mahogany table at the center of the room. Slocum tipped the boy a silver two-bit piece and waited until he closed the door behind him. Pouring coffee into a white china cup, he added a splash of brandy. Underneath a silver serving cover, he found strips of bacon and slices of ham in a dish surrounded by scrambled eggs. A wicker basket of biscuits was covered by a linen cloth. Bowls of strawberry jam and butter rounded out their meal.

Carrying his spiked coffee, he entered the bedroom. Belle slept on her back, magnificent breasts jutting from her rib cage like snow-capped mountains. Her blond curls lay across a pillow in disarray, framing her round face. A bedsheet lay over her stomach, barely covering her from the waist down and for a time he simply stood there, admiring her physical beauty. He'd known her for a number of years, and it seemed as the years passed, she only got prettier. He judged she was close to thirty by now, but her age didn't show in ways he noticed. She became a fiery demon in bed after a couple of bottles of champagne, and no matter how many times he bedded her, he always found it most satisfying. She was one of those rare women who couldn't be fulfilled by a single act of lovemaking. Last night she had demanded that he take her again and again until at last she drifted off to sleep. Perhaps this was one reason why he'd grown so fond of her. Belle had an insatiable appetite for prick. When he entered her she came to a climax almost at once and from that moment on she became one of the most sensual women he'd ever known in bed.

A breeze lifted lace curtains away from a bedroom window and let them drop against the windowsill when the breath of wind died down. Belle stirred, making a tiny fist with one hand to rub her eyes. It was then Slocum noticed her other hand covered by the sheet, and a slow circular motion she made with two fingers she inserted into her cunt while still asleep. Her pelvis began to grind unconsciously against the pressure of her fingers and she gave a soft moan of pleasure.

"She's still hot," Slocum whispered in disbelief. They had made love for hours last night and yet she still wanted more. He found it amazing that any woman could require so much stimulation. Belle was quite a woman, more than most men could satisfy. That, he supposed, was what intrigued him about her. He watched her fingers move faster across the lips of her cunt. Muscles in her legs tightened.

He wondered how she could remain asleep when desire overtook her like this.

A slow smile crossed her face. Her eyelids parted ever so slightly. "You've been watching me," she said huskily. "You thought I was still sleeping, didn't you? How can a woman sleep with a handsome man in the same room? Come to bed, John, and I'll show you how a woman should treat a man first thing in the morning."

"Our breakfast is here, Belle. Aren't you hungry?"

She giggled quietly, playfully. "Hungry for more of your stiff cock, Mr. Slocum." She threw the sheet aside to reveal her cunt and the location of her fingers.

"Our eggs will get cold—"

"To hell with our eggs. I want to feel your balls against my buttocks. We can have eggs another time."

He took another sip of laced coffee and grinned. "You're some woman, Belle. I did my best last night and now you're after more. Remember, I've got a train to catch."

"Come to me, John," she whispered, beckoning to him with wet fingers she withdrew from her cunt. "Make love to me, and do it hard this time. I want something to remember you by. It's too long between your visits to San Antone."

He put his cup down and began unbuttoning his shirt. Seeing her naked, begging him to make love to her, an erection began to pulse inside his pants. Shouldering out of his shirt, he let it fall on the edge of the bed before unfastening his trousers. All the while, Belle continued to rub her fingers around the lips of her mound, moaning softly.

He lay between her milky thighs and licked one pink nipple with the tip of his tongue, then he placed it in his mouth and started to suck on it noisily.

"Oh John!" Belle cried, twisting underneath him, placing her heels behind his knees to draw him close. She reached for his cock and stroked it a few times, until passion got the best of her. She put the head between her moist lips and arched her back while pulling him by the hips. His cock entered her pussy and at once she began feverishly hunching against the base of his shaft, taking every inch of him inside her. She dug her fingernails into the skin of his back and emitted a moan of pure pleasure, rocking under him, squirming, breathing harder and harder.

He took her roughly this time, without any of the gentle attention he gave her last night. Driving his prick into her as hard as he could, their bodies slammed together with increasing frequency until the canopy above the bed shook. Summoning all his power, he stabbed his cock into her cunt as if it were a weapon.

When she reached her release, she let out a wail that he was sure could be heard in the hallway. Her body trembled, frozen in a moment of ecstasy until her climax ebbed away. At last she fell back on the sheet, completely spent, but he was not finished with her yet. Stroking harder, faster, he reached his own climax a moment later and stiffened when his balls emptied in her womb.

When he looked down at Belle, her eyes were glazed over. She smiled. ''That was what I wanted, darling John. Something I can remember during those lonely nights while you're away so long.''

He climbed aboard the passenger car with his valise and war bag under his arm. He waved to Belle as the locomotive whistle sounded. She returned his wave, tilting her black parasol so he could see her face clearly. The black dress she wore revealed so much cleavage that other passengers couldn't help but stare.

Slocum turned into the car and started down a narrow

aisle to find a seat, briefly noting faces of other passengers along the way to see if he recognized anyone. Born out of old habit, he always entered a strange place with the same amount of care, to make certain no one waited for him there who might have an old score to settle.

He found a seat at the rear of the car and put his belongings in a rack above him. He noted that several passengers were watching him, paying attention to his gun belt and the cross-draw holster he wore underneath his black frock coat. Not many men employed a cross-draw rig for their side arms, and he had grown accustomed to a few stares. One gent in particular, a man, seated across the aisle, wearing a brown derby hat and silk vest, paid more attention to Slocum's gun than usual. Slocum settled into his seat and glanced out a window, but when the stranger's stares lasted too long, he turned across the aisle. ''What the hell are you looking at, mister?''

The stranger's face did not change nor did he seem put off by Slocum's tone or the question. ''Your gun,'' he replied. ''I don't see many belly-draw contraptions in my line of work. Just call it simple curiosity.''

There was something about this stranger Slocum didn't like. ''Too damn much curiosity to be polite,'' he said tonelessly. ''I'd hate like hell to have to teach you better manners before this train pulls out.''

Again, there was no change in the man's expression, no show of fear over Slocum's threat. ''That might wind up bein' a tall order, pardner. I figure you believe yourself to be pretty good with that gun or you wouldn't talk so big. In case you're of a mind to wonder, I'm a right decent shot, myself. Unless you're willing to find out who's the better shot, I'd keep those lessons in manners to myself.''

Slocum noticed the bulge of a gun hanging in a shoulder holster inside the stranger's coat; however, the challenge was not the kind of thing he could ignore. Several passengers seated around them overheard what was being said and fell silent, watching the exchange. Slocum grinned at the man across the aisle. In the same instant his right hand jerked his Peacemaker free with a single fluid motion. He sprang from his seat, aiming into the space between the stranger's eyes. The man was still reaching for his pistol when he heard the click of Slocum's Colt being cocked a few inches from his skull. His hand froze.

"You're too damn slow," Slocum hissed. "Now, hand me your gun butt first, or I'll blow a tunnel through your head. One wrong move and somebody'll be scooping up your brains from that platform outside."

"Jesus," the stranger croaked, swallowing, staring into the dark muzzle of Slocum's .44-.40. "Don't shoot me, mister. I was only havin' a little fun." Very carefully, he lifted a small-bore revolver from his coat with thumb and forefinger, holding it out so Slocum could take it. Passengers throughout the noisy car had ended their conversations to watch what was taking place.

Slocum seized the gun and stuck it in his belt. Slowly, he began to relax, realizing that his temper had gotten the best of him. He let the hammer down on his Peacemaker and straightened up, glancing along the aisle. "Trouble's over, folks," he said. "Just a little misunderstanding." He turned back to the stranger and holstered his Colt. "Having a little fun almost cost you your life, mister. If it was me, I'd remember that the next time I found myself in the mood for some fun, 'cause it damn near got you killed." Slocum took a deep breath to calm his nerves. "I want your name, mister, and then tell me about this line of work you say you're in having to do with guns."

"I'm Bo Hollister," he said quietly. "I'm headed down to Laredo to look for a missing woman, a girl. There's a reward posted—"

"I know all about the reward," Slocum told him, mildly surprised to learn that Hollister was traveling to Laredo with the same objective as his own. "I'll be looking for that girl myself. The city marshal at Laredo is a friend of mine. Tom wired me about her. I've got some advice for you, Mr. Hollister, and I suggest you pay real close attention to it. Don't get in my way down there, or the next time I won't let you off so easy. Stay clear of me, or you might not live to regret it."

Slocum sat back down, his anger cooling.

"Sorry," Hollister said, turning his face to a window. He slumped in his seat just as the locomotive began to chug away from the depot.

Slocum felt the other passengers staring at him after the confrontation. He had allowed his temper to get out of hand at the wrong time, promising that it would be a long train ride to Laredo with so many people afraid of him now.

As the depot fell away behind the train, Slocum put his mind on other matters: the captive girl in Mexico and seeing his old friend Tom Spence again. Only once did he consider that Hollister was probably a bounty hunter, or that more men of his ilk were likely to show up around Laredo looking for a chance to earn a big reward. Men like Hollister would only get in the way and there was even a risk they might make the Mexican bandits wary. Slocum knew big money would attract all sorts of desperate men hoping to make ten thousand dollars.

He watched the outskirts of San Antonio pass by the window as the locomotive chugged away from town. From the corner of his eye, he saw Bo Hollister get up and move to another seat to be farther away from him for the long ride to the border. A lesson in better manners had done Hollister a world of good.

4

Slocum rested against the back of a swaying seat, listening to the rhythmic click of train wheels crossing section joints in the tracks, remembering Tom Spence and the war. A hot, sooty wind blew in his face from the passenger car window. He paid no attention to mile after empty mile of mesquite brushland through which the train labored, for his mind was elsewhere, back to a bloody battle at Manassas where he first met Tom, a boy about the same age as he, barely seventeen.

Although they both served in the Calhoun County Militia, they were from different parts of the Allegheny Mountains and hadn't met until the militia, commanded by John's father, William Slocum, was called to war when the state of Georgia joined other secessionist states in the summer of 1860. John's older brother, Robert, rode off with them to fight Yankees. Robert was killed in 1863 after just being commissioned a lieutenant prior to the battle at Gettysburg in a charge led by Thomas "Stonewall" Jackson. Jackson earned his nickname at Manassas, called the battle of Bull Run. Jackson's Brigade was known throughout the Confederacy for its courage, a reputation that probably cost Robert Slocum his life. Robert was at the front of Pickett's charge in the battle for Little

Round Top. John was assigned to the sharpshooters covering the charge and that fact, that he was a superior marksman, had most likely been the reason his life was spared that fateful day at Gettysburg. With a Spencer rifle, his aim was almost perfect.

Fighting alongside him, young Tom Spence was also a crack shot, cutting down men in blue as fast as he could reload. After that terrible experience, he and Tom were all but inseparable, until General Lee made John a courier to General Sterling Price after Grant's victory at Vicksburg. Now that the Union controlled the Mississippi, General Price had to fight a different war in the west. "Bloody Kansas," as it was called, had been turned into a gory battleground by Union Jayhawkers and Confederate Redlegs. Quantrill led a band of Confederates so ruthless that Richmond severed relations with them. Burning and looting became so commonplace that neither side observed a code of honor. John was promoted to the rank of captain by General Price, assigning him to Quantrill.

It was with the madman Quantrill that John Slocum learned mastery of the Colt revolver, and also where he developed an attitude toward fighting and death that was to become a part of his nature for the balance of his lifetime. It was when he was with Quantrill at Lawrence, Kansas, where Slocum caught a bullet that nearly killed him. It was months later, in the spring of 1866, after the war ended, before Slocum was well enough to travel, returning home to find his father and mother both dead, his farm seized for back taxes by the new carpetbagger government in reconstruction Georgia. It was at the family farm where he killed his first men out of uniform, a gunman hired to enforce carpetbagger policies in Calhoun County and a county judge who came to serve papers on the Slocum farm. With warrants out for his arrest, Slocum had put a torch to the place and ridden west to escape bitter memories and a death sentence.

The passenger car rocked, awakening Slocum from thoughts of his past. He stared out the window, thinking about Tom Spence and a happy reunion between them when he got to Laredo. If Tom wanted, they might talk about the war for a while, but if Slocum had his way, they wouldn't discuss it. It was a time he wanted to forget. The war had cost him his family and their homestead, and had given him a terrible scar as a reminder of how close he'd come to death. He remembered reading somewhere that over six hundred thousand men had died on both sides— he'd seen the bloated corpses at Manassas and in the Shenandoah Valley, and finally at Gettysburg. It made no sense to talk about what they'd seen back then, what they'd gone through together. Slocum was sure Tom remembered it as vividly as he did, occasionally robbing him of sleep when dreams about those times awakened him in a cold sweat.

The train slowed near a water tower in the midst of a bald mesquite prairie to take on water and firewood for the boiler. A clapboard shack sat beside the tracks and behind it, an old wagon drawn by a rawboned gray mule sat in the shade of an eave. A boy in white cotton pants waited with a box of sandwiches and a masonry jar advertising lemonade. As soon as the locomotive ground to a halt, the boy climbed into the first passenger car to peddle his wares. Passengers got up to stretch and make use of a small two-door outhouse behind the shack. But as Slocum was coming to his feet, he saw Bo Hollister coming over, and by the look on his face there was something on his mind.

"Look, mister, I'm powerful sorry for what I said a while ago," Hollister began. "I'd sure like to get my gun back, if it's all the same to you."

Slocum's eyes narrowed. "What'll keep you from trying your luck again, maybe when my back's turned?"

"You've got my word I won't do no such thing," he replied, eyes darting to the butt of his pistol stuck in the waistband of Slocum's pants.

"Why would I think your word is any good, Hollister? You don't strike me as any kind of honorable man. You wanted to goad me into a gunfight when I got on this train—"

"I gave you an honest apology for that. There ain't a hell of a lot more a man can do besides give his word."

Slocum was still sizing him up. "I'll think on it some," he said, sounding doubtful.

Hollister appeared to be encouraged. "Maybe the two of us can strike a bargain of some kind, maybe go in partners to look for that girl down in Mexico, split the reward two ways."

"I always work alone, Mr. Hollister. Besides, as slow as you are going for your gun, you probably wouldn't live long down below the border. That neck of the woods is full of hard cases who'd blow your brains out for the boots you're wearing. I've spent some time down in Tamaulipas and Coahuila. There's a man on damn near every street corner who'd kill you for the price of a jug of tequila. Forget about us forming any sort of partnership. It ain't in my deck of cards."

Now Hollister was a little put off. "You ain't had a chance to see what I can do, mister. I can read hoofprints the way some men read a newspaper an' I'm something of an expert on explosives, if I do say so myself. I've got some dynamite packed in a box in the baggage car. Dynamite is liable to come in real handy if you find the Mexicans who took her holed up someplace."

Slocum frowned. "Dynamite could also kill the girl."

"Not if the man who uses it knows what he's doin'. I

got a lot of experience workin' with explosives. I done the dynamitin' for several mining companies in Colorado. I know how to make a hole in solid rock the size of a man's head, or I can bring down half a mountain if I take a mind to. If those Mexicans take a notion to fortify themselves someplace, dynamite's the only way to blast 'em out. And I know how to use a rifle. I've made a pretty fair livin' huntin' down wanted men in the territories of late.''

"You're a bounty hunter," Slocum observed dryly, having a dislike for men of that persuasion.

"Some call it that," Hollister agreed. "I go after men the law can't find themselves. I'm usually pretty successful at it."

"You're damn sure slow on the draw," Slocum remembered.

"Never claimed to be no professional shootist. I had you figured for a gambler, by the cut of your fancy suit. I got no use for cardsharps an' that's what you looked like to me. I said I was sorry for what I said, for what happened. I was wrong. I misjudged you."

It was a risk, but Slocum took out Hollister's pistol and handed it back to him. "You can keep your gun, but if you reach for it again when I'm around, I swear I'll kill you dead as a fence post."

Hollister took his revolver and returned it to his shoulder holster. "What about the chances of a partnership between you an' me? Two sets of eyes are better'n one."

"I'll think on it some, but I'd call it highly unlikely. I told you before that I work alone."

"I'd carry my share of the load. We'd make a good team, you an' me."

"I doubt it," Slocum remarked, "but you're entitled to your opinion."

Hollister glanced over his shoulder as the boy selling

food and drinks came down the aisle. "Let me buy you a sandwich and a glass of lemonade. We'll talk over lunch."

Slocum wagged his head. "No thanks. I never drink lemonade, and I'm not in the habit of eating with strangers who try to pull a gun on me."

"I said I was sorry 'bout that. I had you figured wrong."

"After I have a talk with Marshal Spence at Laredo, I'll know more about what I'm up against. If I think there's any need for a man who knows explosives, I'll look you up. Until then, consider the matter closed. I'm not looking for any partners."

Hollister's face fell as Slocum turned to leave the train to stretch his legs. Slocum knew it was a gamble, turning his back on a man who'd gone for a gun against him a few hours ago, but he had Hollister judged for a cowardly man who wouldn't take another chance like that unless he was convinced he couldn't lose.

When Slocum climbed down from the car, he gave the surrounding dry brushland a passing examination. Everything that grew in south Texas had thorns. Slender mesquite trees had razorlike spines on every branch and beds of cactus lying everywhere were bristling with needles. Rare tufts of dry buffalo grass grew in small clumps between the mesquites and cactus. It was a no-man's-land if ever there was one, and this was what most of northern Mexico was like. The ground was powder dry. Water for men and horses would be scarce. Without knowledge of where to find rare waterholes, a man could die of thirst in a matter of days.

Slocum sauntered over to the woodshed and rested in the shade to escape the blistering sun. He wondered how he would fare crossing land like this on the back of a horse. It would be one hell of a test of horseflesh, requiring that he purchase a range-bred animal wise to the ways of a desert. Tom could help him with that. If he decided to go at all. It would depend on what he could learn about the bandits' territory and places they were known to frequent. Without getting good information ahead of time, he would be looking for a needle in a haystack down there.

He watched trainmen drain water from a wooden tower into the belly of the locomotive. Without precious water, not even a train could manage this brutal land. A well or a river would be the lifeblood those bandits needed. Learning where to find water in the region he had to cross was his first order of business if he agreed to take the job.

He thought back to Bo Hollister. Hollister was untrustworthy, Slocum was sure of that. But a time might come when a man who knew explosives could come in handy. On a few occasions in the past, Slocum had made deals with the devil's own representatives in order to accomplish his objectives.

The train whistle sounded, announcing time for passengers to reboard. He pushed away from the woodshed wall and walked slowly back to the car. According to a conductor he had asked, they should make it to Laredo before midnight if the locomotive or loose tracks didn't give any unforseen delays.

Slocum took his seat by a rear window, after taking off his coat to escape the sweltering heat. He laid the coat beside him and tilted his hat over his eyes, making sure that Bo Hollister was in another part of the car. Earlier, Slocum had noticed a young woman aboard the train, a brunette with rouge on her cheeks and painted red lips. She wore a gray gown buttoned high on her neck, presenting a very proper and ladylike appearance. But once in a while he caught her staring at him, although she always looked away quickly when their eyes met. She was a pretty woman, and given the chance he would like to get to know her.

The locomotive belched steam and slowly chugged away from the water tower. Keeping his hat brim low over his eyes, Slocum admired the woman in secret, savouring the swell of her breasts inside her dress and the delicate curve of her ankles where her stockings showed beneath the hem of her gown. Soon the train labored to full speed, pounding its way south amid a cloud of black soot pouring from the smokestack.

Later, Slocum noticed the woman take out a paper fan and begin fanning herself. The seat beside her was vacant and he pondered his chances of joining her in the empty seat. But if she had witnessed the exchange between himself and Hollister, it was unlikely she would invite him to sit beside her. It was an unfortunate incident, but one that couldn't be helped.

As the sun set, cooler air flowed into the windows of the car. The pretty brunette put her fan away and adjusted her skirt across the hard wood seat. Then she looked up at Slocum and caught him watching her. She gave him a slight smile and a polite nod before she looked the other way.

"I might get lucky," he whispered to himself. Her smile had been an outright invitation, he thought.

A few more minutes passed before Slocum put on his coat and tugged down the cuffs of his sleeves, making himself as presentable as possible. He stood up and reached into his valise for a pint of good Kentucky whiskey he'd purchased for the trip. If he offered the lady a drink, he hoped she wouldn't be offended.

5

The interior of the car had begun to darken after sunset as Slocum made his way up the gently rocking aisle carrying his pint of sour mash whiskey. He paused in front of the woman and tipped his hat, giving her a friendly grin. "A pleasant evening, ma'am. I wondered if you might care to join me in a drink of bourbon. I hope I'm not being too forward. Allow me to introduce myself. My name is John Slocum. Would you care for a drink?"

She had been watching him from the moment he left his seat. A look of concern crossed her face, then it disappeared. "I do not usually imbibe with strangers, Mr. Slocum. I was a witness to that rather ugly incident with the other passenger, and I must say that you seem to be quite a rogue. It hardly seems proper for a woman of good breeding to sit and drink liquor with a total stranger who threatened another passenger with a pistol."

Slocum liked the sound of her voice. "That was an unfortunate occurrence, one that I sincerely regret. However, the man was insisting upon a confrontation. I never meant to shoot him, only to teach him some better manners. I can assure you that I'm not the rogue you think I am. Given the opportunity, I feel sure I can convince you otherwise."

34

A playful smile lifted the corners of her ruby lips. "I may have been wrong about you, Mr. Slocum. My name is Dora Fitzgerald. I'm a schoolteacher on my way to a teaching assignment in Laredo at the Normal School for Girls. I suppose no harm will come from sharing a small drink with you. Please do sit down."

He accepted her invitation and took a seat opposite hers as the conductor came into the car to light the oil lamps. A few of the other passengers watched him sit down with the woman, including Bo Hollister, although they turned their heads quickly when he cast a glance their way. He uncorked the bottle and offered it to her with an apology. "No glasses, I'm afraid, Miss Fitzgerald. Sorry."

She took his whiskey and sipped from the neck, making a face after she tasted it. "It's quite strong, isn't it?"

"You get used to it."

"I only drink whiskey for its medicinal qualities. I must admit my nerves are a little on edge over my teaching assignment in Laredo. I've been told Laredo is a very rowdy town." She put the bottle to her lips and drank again, a larger swallow.

"The city marshal is an old friend of mine. If you wish, I can introduce you to him, just in case you ever have need of the marshal's services."

"That would be very nice," Dora said, returning the bottle to him. She examined his face more closely in the light from the oil lamps. "I'm curious as to your line of work, Mr. Slocum, and the fact that you feel the need to carry a gun."

He drank a generous swallow himself and sat back against his seat. "In recent years I've done some detective work for some of the railroads. Train robberies have been on the increase around the Denver area. I'm on my way to Laredo to help investigate the disappearance of a young woman. She was apparently abducted by a gang of Mexican bandits who've taken her into Mexico. My friend, the city marshal, wired me to come down for a talk with him and the father of the girl. A fairly sizable reward has been offered for the girl's safe return, since those bandits are beyond the reach of Texas law south of the border.''

"There is no law in Mexico?"

He chuckled. "Not much, I'm afraid. The Mexican government is in a state of chaos right now. A revolution is brewing, and it keeps them busy. I'll be acting on my own, unofficially, if I go down there to try to arrange for the girl's release.''

"It sounds very dangerous. You must be a brave man to take that sort of chance.''

Slocum grew more fascinated with Dora as time passed. She was, indeed, a beautiful woman. Emerald eyes watched him from a face of flawless ivory. "I've never considered myself a particularly brave sort. Careful is a better word. I don't take big chances unless I calculate the risks beforehand. If I believe I can get the girl back to her father unharmed, I'll make the attempt, but only when I'm convinced I stand a good chance of getting it done safely.''

"It still sounds very courageous. Something could go wrong.''

"I try to allow for that. Being prepared is the best remedy for most unexpected surprises.'' He drank again and offered her the pint.

Dora took the bottle and swallowed a more liberal amount this time. Outside the passenger car window, darkness settled over thorny brushland like a black blanket. She puckered some when the whiskey burned her throat. "In spite of the terrible taste, I do feel more relaxed now,'' she told him. Her green eyes came to meet his. "Do you have a family, Mr. Slocum?''

He wagged his head. "My father and brother were

killed in the war. My mother died of grief afterward, or so I was told. She was dead before I could get home from Kansas. I was wounded in a fight with some Jayhawkers just as the war was coming to a close. I've never had a wife or children. I suppose I never found a woman who could tolerate my wanderlust. I get this urge to see the other side of a mountain, sometimes. I've been on the move a lot since the war.''

Dora's eyes sparkled in the lamplight. ''Maybe you never found the right woman who understood you.''

''I reckon that's a possibility. Not many women will abide long absences from a man.'' As he was thinking about the truth of what he said, he was listening to the distant chug of the engine. ''Maybe the right woman just hasn't come along yet,'' he added with a grin. ''I haven't given up looking . . .''

She reached for the pint of whiskey and drank from it as the train rounded a curve. Slocum thought he noticed a hint of color in her cheeks.

''I have arranged for a room at a boarding house in Laredo,'' she said. ''It's close to the school. Perhaps, if you have time and the inclination, you could pay me a social call there. It's called Grayson's, on Santa Maria Road.''

He knew the whiskey was loosening her up now. ''When we get to Laredo, I'll be glad to escort you there in a rented carriage. Laredo can be a dangerous city late at night.''

Dora's blush deepened. ''Why, that would be quite gentlemanly of you, Mr. Slocum. I'll gladly pay for the carriage. I have some money, a small amount.''

''That won't be necessary, Miss Fitzgerald. I'd planned to rent a carriage to carry my own belongings to my hotel. We can ask for directions to Grayson's as soon as we get to town.''

She gave him a very different look then. "I must admit I was wrong about you, Mr. Slocum, believing you were something of a rogue. You are truly a gentleman who wouldn't take advantage of a woman traveling alone."

He rested a booted foot across his knee. "It never crossed my mind to take unfair advantage of a lady," he told her, noting that almost half the whiskey was gone.

The train steamed across a stretch of flat prairie. Slocum judged they were still two hours from Laredo.

Dora was decidedly drunk, unable to stand without assistance when he held her by the arm. He guided her up the stairs to his room at the Posada Hotel. She giggled every now and then when she lost her balance on the steps. Escorting her down a darkened hallway with a young Mexican boy carrying her trunk and suitcase, he hoped Dora wasn't too drunk to enjoy the rest of the evening. Unlocking his door, he instructed the boy as to where to put her belongings and paid him a quarter. As soon as the door was shut, he helped Dora to the edge of the bed and lit a lantern.

"It's hot in here," she gasped, unfastening the top button on her dress. "Please open a window. Perhaps it's the whiskey making me feel so warm."

He opened a window and took off his coat, then he came to the bed and offered her the last swallow of whiskey. She took it and sighed.

"Let me help you out of your dress so you'll be cooler," he suggested, opening another button, and yet another.

"Please turn down the lantern," she whispered throatily, a faraway look in her eyes. "I really shouldn't be doing this. It's so unladylike to undress in front of a strange man. We scarcely know each other at all."

He bent down and kissed her lightly on the lips. "We

know each other well enough, Dora, and this room is so terribly hot.''

She assented by nodding once while he continued to unfasten her buttons. He drew her gown over her milky shoulders and let it fall to her waist. Then he kissed her again, longer this time and with more passion. A quiet moan came from her throat. She reached for a drawstring gathering her corset in front and untied it. Her ample breasts strained to be free of the fabric and as she opened the front where it was joined, her bosom mushroomed to a size even Slocum had not predicted. Her breasts were large, well formed, rising firmly from her chest. Her nipples were small, pink, and twisted into hard little knots.

''Please turn down the lantern,'' she asked again, trying to cover her naked breasts with small hands. ''It isn't proper for a man to see a woman like this.''

He reached for the wick and lowered its flame until the room was almost dark. Then he kissed her again and started taking off his shirt.

''Oh, John,'' Dora whispered, when he drew his mouth away.

Gently, he laid her across the mattress and pulled her dress over her hips, leaving her wearing nothing but her stockings and high-button shoes. He removed his gun belt, then his boots and pants. When he lay down beside her, he could hear her breathing hard, and he could smell her perfume. Carefully, he put his arms around her and drew her body against his.

''I don't want you to think I'm some kind of trollop,'' she said softly. ''I've never done this sort of thing with a total stranger. But you are so ruggedly handsome, and the whiskey has made me forget that I'm a schoolteacher. Please be gentle with me, John. I'm not very experienced . . .''

He cupped one breast in his hand. Kissing her lightly

on her neck, he whispered, "I promise I'll be gentle."

She crossed one shapely leg over his hips, bringing her soft mound close to his belly. Slocum ran a hand down her thigh to her knee, then up the curve of her leg to her buttocks.

"Oh John!" Dora gasped, when she felt his erection touch her abdomen.

He curled his fingers into the moist lips of her cunt and left them there, feeling her warmth. She began to breathe harder in short, rapid bursts. For now he'd forgotten all about a girl being held prisoner by Mexican bandidos. Tonight he was finding rapture in the arms of Dora Fitzgerald, and business would have to wait until morning.

He entered her, very slowly, very carefully, so as not to hurt her. When his prick slid inside her, she shuddered and bit her lip to keep from crying out. An inch at a time he pushed his shaft into her, until it felt as if there were no more room for him there.

Reflexively, Dora began to hunch against him, tentatively at first, groaning each time she thrust against the base of his thick member.

He matched every upward push of her groin with pressure of his own, feeling her muscles tighten, listening to her soft moans of pleasure. The bed began to rock. Outside his hotel window all was quiet in the streets of Laredo, for the hour was late, well past midnight. Very gradually, the tempo of their lovemaking increased and now metal bedsprings made a cracking sound with every movement they made. Dora's moans became louder and, to stifle them, she gently bit the lobe of his right ear.

His balls exploded inside her a quarter hour later, after the woman's second climax. They fell asleep in each other's arms and slept soundly until dawn.

6

Tom Spence looked much older than Slocum expected. Tom's face sported a gray handlebar mustache and his sideburns were graying. Slocum didn't bother to count the years since they'd seen each other, nearly twenty by his rough guess. Entering the city marshal's office, he almost didn't recognize the man seated at a rolltop desk against one wall.

"Is that you, Tom?" he asked, closing the door behind him.

Tom's face broke into a wide grin. "It's me, all right. I would have known you anywhere, John Slocum. Wouldn't have needed to ask." He got up quickly and strode across the room to shake Slocum's hand. "Damn, Johnny boy, it's mighty good to see you. Been a long time since we had a handshake. Last time I remember was when Gen'l Lee sent you to Kansas. I was half scared I'd never set eyes on you again, after I heard Price assigned you to Quantrill's bunch. It's a rotten dirty shame we ain't kept in touch with each other. Partly my fault, I reckon, only I did find out you was workin' as a railroad detective up in Denver."

"That was a few months back. I've been in Fort Worth

41

for a spell, tryin' to find out who's been robbing the Texas
Pacific. I got your wire after a friend at the marshal's
office in Denver had the message sent to me. I got here
as quickly as I could.''

"Take a seat," Tom suggested, pointing to a leather
chair beside the desk, still grinning from ear to ear. "I've
got coffee made. I'll pour you a cup an' we'll catch up
on things."

Slocum took the chair Tom offered. "Not much to tell,
Tom. I've been working for the railroads for a while. Handled a few other odd jobs, traveling around a bit seeing
places I've never seen. I've been making a living, I
reckon."

Tom went over to a potbellied stove where a smoke-
blackened coffeepot gave off mouthwatering smells. He
took a tin cup off a peg near the stove and poured coffee.
"I'm mighty glad you came, Johnny, only you may wish
you hadn't wasted your time after I tell you everything
about what happened to the Anderson girl." He carried
the cup over and handed it to Slocum. "She was taken
prisoner by one of the worst border outlaws in recent
memory. A man by the name of Victoriano Valdez. He
leads a small revolutionary army hiding out in the Sierras
down near Saltillo. I'd call him a cross between a patriot
and a thief. He's been on the run for half a dozen years,
dodging Federales all over the place. This is the first time
he's ever crossed the border to pull one of his raids."
Tom returned to his chair, giving the office wall a
thoughtful stare. "I've notified the Federale commandant
in Nuevo Laredo and informed the Texas Rangers. But as
you might have guessed, nobody's doin' anything about
the missing girl. I can tell you that Howard Anderson
wants to talk to you about how you'll go about finding
his daughter. And the reward's real. I can show you written authorization from the Cattleman's Bank to pay ten

thousand dollars to whoever brings Melissa back here safe an' sound. This town's been crawlin' with sleazy types who claim they'll get her back if half the reward's paid up front. I told Howard that would be a fool's move. There's been better'n twenty men showed up to inquire about the money, and I'm sure more are on the way.''

"One of 'em is named Bo Hollister," Slocum said. "I met him on the train from San Antone last night. I don't figure he's all that much of a risk-taker. If the job looks easy, he'll make a play for the reward. Otherwise, he won't make a move."

"Every no-account saddle tramp in this part of Texas asks me about the money, but not one of 'em looks like a man who can get the job done. If there's a way to find her, I know you'll be the one to do it. But I can promise you it'll be tricky. Victoriano Valdez is a ruthless cutthroat an' he ain't nobody to fool around with, Johnny. He's just about the meanest son of a bitch in this part of the country. If he thinks you're onto him, he'll slit her throat an' likely make things rough for whoever gets too close to him."

Slocum had been thinking while Tom was talking. "Will Valdez listen to an offer of ransom? If the girl's father offered him a chunk of money for her safe return, would Valdez listen?"

"Hard to say," Tom remarked, rubbing his chin. "Money can do powerful things, but nobody knows Valdez well enough to figure out how his mind works.

Slocum considered it more thoroughly. "How tough would it be to contact him without getting my head shot off?"

Tom shrugged. "It'd only be a guess, but Valdez might think it's a trick of some kind, figuring he'd be walkin' into a trap. If he suspicioned he was bein' set up, he'll be twice as dangerous."

"If there was someone he trusted—"

"Men like Valdez don't trust nobody, usually."

Slocum took a sip of coffee when an unexpected recollection of the time he spent with Dora Fitzgerald entered his thoughts. She had been so embarrassed this morning when she awoke beside him at the hotel. Finding herself completely naked, she covered her body with a sheet and started to cry, blaming whiskey for her unabashed behavior. He was finally able to comfort her enough so she could get dressed without shedding more tears. On the drive out to her boarding house, she'd begun crying again. He'd halted the rented carriage under a live oak tree long enough to convince her that she'd done nothing wrong, that two people met and shared a special evening together. He promised to call on her again as soon as his business in Laredo was finished and that seemed to console her somewhat.

"I met a beautiful lady on the train, Tom, a schoolteacher by the name of Dora Fitzgerald. If she ever needs help, I'd be obliged if you'd see what you can do for her."

Tom chuckled. "That part of your disposition ain't changed none over the years. You always was quite the ladies' man. Did you ever take a wife?"

Slocum shook his head. "How about you?"

"I got married to Maria a few months after the war was over. We met in a roadhouse close to Memphis. She's a Mexican girl an' Laredo was her home. That's how come I wound up here. Followed her back an' we got hitched. We've got four kids, nearly all of 'em grown up an' moved off. Time sure has passed since you an' me last saw each other. We've got a lot of catchin' up to do."

"I'd just as soon not talk about the war. I've tried real hard to forget it."

Tom nodded. "Me, too. There's some things we hadn't

oughta remember. Good to know you feel the same way . . .''

Slocum drank more coffee. "I suppose the first thing is for me to meet this Howard Anderson. When can you arrange it?"

"Right now, if that suits you. Howard wanted to talk to you as soon as you arrived, after I told him you'd answered my wire. He's a mighty sorrowful man right now, Johnny. That girl means everything to him—she's all he has. Melissa's mother died when she was giving birth to her. Howard's all torn up inside over what those men will do to his daughter. She's real pretty, not quite eighteen years old. A man don't need much imagination to guess what they'll do."

"Let's drive out to Anderson's. I rented a buggy at the livery stable. If I decide to head into Mexico to look for this Valdez, I'll need a horse that's wise to the desert."

Tom stood up, wincing a little, as though his knees gave him pain. "I've got a good blue roan gelding I'll loan you. Stout as a red Missouri mule when it comes to packin' a load, and he can run. He was raised on a ranch west of here and he's bred for this type of dry country."

Slocum got up, and that was when Tom noticed his gun.

"I see you carry a Peacemaker. Damn reliable gun, but I never did cotton to drawin' across my belly like that."

"It took a little getting used to," Slocum agreed, following Tom out the office door while taking note of the pistol Tom carried, a .44 caliber Mason Colt conversion tied low on his right leg. "I see you prefer a Mason."

Tom locked the door behind them. "Damn near any side arm is better than them Dance pistols the Confederacy issued. Worst gun to misfire ever was made, unless you count them early Walkers. I got me a bellyful of misfires durin' the war. Made myself take an oath I'd never own another unreliable shootin' iron. In my profession, a feller can't afford but one mistake. I wouldn't trade this Mason Colt for all the pistols in the world.''

Slocum led the way to his carriage and climbed in the front seat. Tom was a little slower on his bad knees making it up.

"Head southwest along the river," Tom instructed, pointing with a gnarled finger that appeared to have been broken sometime in the past. "I'll show you some pretty scenery on the way out to the ranch. This summer the river bottom's been green. We've had a respectable amount of rain, which ain't usual for most of Webb County.''

Slocum turned the buggy horse and slapped the reins over its back, driving off in a cloud of yellow caliche dust rising between rows of small stores and shops. A few people were out and about on the streets, although it was early, before ten o'clock. He saw a side street lined with saloons and cantinas on their way out of town, remembering that district as the toughest part of Laredo. Tom Spence had one hell of a job to handle here and the simple fact that he was still alive serving as a lawman on the Mexican border was proof enough that he knew how to take care of himself in a tight spot.

Leaving town down a rutted road running beside the Rio Grande, Slocum admired big cottonwoods along the river's edge, and occasionally, drooping willows grew on the banks. Grass was abundant, making the river an oasis passing through one of the worst stretches of desert in the entire Southwest. Water gave life to the land. The Rio Grande was the only reason towns like Laredo and Del Rio and Eagle Pass could exist. But the river was much more than water, it was a magic boundary beyond which men wanted by the law couldn't be touched. Just south of the river desperados of every description lived beyond the reach of warrants for their arrest from most every state in the Union. Slocum remembered the frustration he heard from Texas Rangers who had trailed their quarry hundreds of miles, only to be forced to give up and turn back on the banks of this river. If Slocum decided to cross it, he would have no legal authority whatsoever, and only by living by his wits could he hope to stay alive.

"Looks mighty peaceful, don't it?" Tom asked, sighting down the Rio Grande's lush banks. "What most men don't realize is that just over yonder lies a haven for every type of sorry son of a bitch on earth. A blindfolded man could throw a rock most any direction an' be damn sure of hittin' a wanted outlaw two out of three times."

Slocum chuckled softly over the example Tom used, but in his heart he knew just how right Tom was. Crossing that river was tantamount to entering a war zone.

Following the Rio Grande for about five miles, Slocum and Tom swung off to the northwest down a pair of dim wagon ruts that would take them to the Anderson Ranch headquarters. Slocum wasn't prepared to see a mansion surrounded by tall cottonwood trees out in the middle of a desert choked with thorny brush, but that's what he found when they came in sight of the sprawling hacienda belonging to Howard Anderson, a rambling adobe home surrounded by a low adobe wall. Several bunkhouses and adobe shacks sat behind the main house, a place for vaqueros and ranch hands to live, he judged. The ranch was almost a small city, a collection of buildings impressive to any casual traveler who happened to pass this way for the first time.

Slocum guided the brown harness horse toward an opening in the wall leading into a courtyard. Well-tended gardens and all manner of bright flowers grew inside the wall. Chickens pecked across the courtyard, scattering from the buggy wheels when they drove up to the front of the house. When the buggy came to a halt, a man dressed in a dark suit coat and trousers came out the front door.

"Howard," Tom began, stepping gingerly from the buggy to the ground, "this here's the man I told you about, Mr. John Slocum. I brought him out just as soon as he got to town so the two of you could talk."

Slocum got down to shake with a lean, rawboned man of forty whose darkened skin showed the effects of long hours in the sun, and whose callused hands were not unfamiliar with hard work. His handshake was firm, yet brief.

"I like the looks of you, Mr. Slocum. Tom's told me a great deal about you. I'm sure he's filled you in on what happened here last week. The bastards have taken my daughter, and I'm offering ten thousand dollars to anyone who can get her back. I'd like to hear what you have to say. Please step inside out of the sun. I have whiskey an' good cigars."

Slocum nodded. "I've got some ideas. Can't say for sure if they'll work or not, but I figure there's only a couple of ways to get your daughter back alive."

"Come inside," Howard said, leading the way to his front door with a Winchester rifle balanced in his left fist. He was bowlegged, Slocum noted, proving that he was no stranger to a horse and saddle.

They entered a cool tiled hallway and walked into a dark room with windows covered by thick drapery to keep out the sun. Howard pointed them to thick upholstered chairs before he went to a side bar where rows of bottles were arranged behind glasses. "Name your poison, Mr. Slocum," Howard said. "I know Tom prefers good corn squeeze, but I've got brandy and the best tequila money can buy."

Slocum settled into a comfortable chair. "I'll try some of that tequila. And you made mention of good cigars . . ." He could tell by the expensive look of everything else that the tobacco would be some of the best. While Howard was pouring, Slocum made ready to outline his plan to arrange for Melissa's return . . . if she were still alive, which was anybody's guess until there was proof one way or another.

7

Howard Anderson took a chair after drinks and cigars were passed out to his guests. He drank a healthy swallow of whiskey, and when he brought the glass to his lips his hand was shaking. Then he gave Slocum another careful look of appraisal. "Tom said you did some detective work for the railroad."

"Some," Slocum replied, tasting his tequila and finding it to be gentler than most varieties. "Train robberies have been on the rise around Denver. There've also been some problems with the Texas Pacific near Fort Worth." He lit the cheroot and drew in sweet smoke. Howard Anderson believed in having the best money could buy.

"Tom tells me you can handle yourself with a gun. I figure there'll be plenty of gunplay getting my daughter back, if it can be done at all. I'm quite sure you'll need to hire a few extra gunhands, Mr. Slocum. Valdez surrounds himself with *pistoleros* who know their business."

"There might be another way," Slocum offered. "Valdez might be willing to sell her back to you, so to speak, if the money's right. I see it as a safer gamble for your daughter's sake. If he's like all the rest of Mexico's bandits, he's more interested in money."

Howard scowled. "I'm real disappointed hearin' you say that you want me to negotiate with those bastards. That just ain't my way of doing business. I aimed to teach that son of a bitch a lesson for what he did to me. He killed thirteen of my cowboys and took my daughter hostage—"

"If you want your daughter back unharmed, I suggest you try to negotiate with him first. Trying to settle a score with guns could easily get her killed. As soon as the first shot is fired, he's liable to kill her. If we offer him money, I think there's a better chance he'll let her go. A revolution has to have guns and bullets. Those things cost money."

Howard's frown deepened. "Hell, Slocum, I'm offering ten thousand dollars. Looks like that oughta be enough to raise an army of mercenaries. You find him and surround him with enough hired gunmen, and he'll see his goose is cooked."

"Maybe. Or it could work another way. He might slice her throat. Are you willing to take that chance in order to have a taste of revenge?"

At that, the rancher's eyes wavered. "No," he said quietly before he gulped more whiskey. "Tell me more about your idea."

Slocum glanced at Tom before he continued. "If I agree to take an offer of five thousand dollars in gold to this Valdez for the safe return of your girl, it'll cost you five more for me to take the risks. That way, it's the same money to you. Five goes to me if I'm successful, and the five thousand in gold is paid to Valdez. It stands a chance of working, a far better chance than hiring a small army of paid shootists to go down there looking for trouble. It's been my experience that a man can find all the trouble he wants south of the Rio Grande. The Federales won't lift a hand to help an American, and there sure as hell are plenty of desperados who'll trade lead with anybody who takes a notion to start shooting.''

By the look on Howard's face he still wasn't too keen on a peaceful settlement. ''That don't punish him for what he did to my cowboys. Thirteen good men lie buried in the ground because of him. Some left wives and children behind.'' He sighed deeply and drained his glass. ''But what you say makes sense. I want Melissa back more'n anything in the whole world. The ranch, my money, nothing matters more than her. She's all the family I have and I've got to get her back somehow, some way. I'll spend every last cent I own to have her brought back to me. Offer that rotten bastard Valdez as much as it takes to buy her back for me and I'll pay you five thousand dollars, besides your expenses. It sticks in my craw like sand to have to pay him, but I reckon I'll do it to have her home safe. There'll come another day for me and him to settle our affairs. I'm a man who believes in an eye for an eye. But I won't argue that your way is better for Melissa's sake. Let's offer the bastard money.''

''I think it's a better idea than trying to shoot my way in, and there's no guarantee that money will work, either. But I'll make the try. Finding him and getting to talk to him is going to be the hardest part.''

''John's idea makes the most sense,'' Tom said. ''And if there is any trouble, he'll know how to handle it. The most important thing is Melissa's safety. Getting her back a peaceful way will be the smartest, if Valdez will listen.''

Howard arched one eyebrow. He looked at Slocum. ''What will happen if he won't take money?''

Slocum considered his answer carefully before he gave it. ''I won't have any choice then but to employ other means. If he won't listen to a reasonable ransom offer, then maybe he'll have to listen to other types of persuasion.''

Tom gave Slocum a mirthless grin. "Like those Yank bastards at Little Round Top that time . . ."

A silence followed. Howard seemed to be debating himself. After a moment, he spoke to Tom. "Inform the others who've made inquiries that the reward has been withdrawn. I'm betting on Mr. Slocum. Spread the word around that someone has been hired to do the job. Frankly, the ones I've seen don't appear to be worth a dose of salts. Most of 'em are just saddle bums who own a gun."

Tom agreed. "You've got the best man, Howard. Me and John have been through some tough times together an' when the chips are down, you can count on him. If it was my daughter, I'd rather have John Slocum lookin' for her than anybody else I ever knew."

"That's good enough for me," Howard said. He got up to pour fresh drinks. "How soon can you leave, Mr. Slocum?" He picked up a tequila bottle and added a splash to Slocum's glass.

"Finding out which direction to go is the first thing. Tom tells me Valdez is known to frequent the Sierra foot-hills down around Saltillo. I'll need better information, but I may have a way of finding out a little more tonight. Tom's loaning me a horse."

"I've got plenty of horses," Howard said. "You can have the pick of my string."

"I might take along a spare for a couple of reasons. If I get your daughter back, she'll need a good animal under her for a quick ride to the border, and there's also a chance that I might cripple a horse in rough country if somebody pushes me. You can pick a good dry-country horse for me to take along. Other than my guns and a few staples, I'll be traveling pretty light so I can cover some ground." He knocked back tequila as soon as he'd said all he needed to say, enjoying the soft burn down his throat into his belly. The rancher offered him another shot and he took it gladly, puffing on his cigar while Howard added whiskey to his own glass and Tom's.

"What'll you do about runnin' the ranch, Howard?" Tom asked. "I reckon you need to hire a new crew of vaqueros."

Howard sank back down in his chair. "I've already hired two men from the Rafter Y, extra hands Yancy Wardlaw didn't need. I can use half a dozen more before the fall roundup, so if you see any good men lookin' for day work, send them out to see me. It won't be the same, after losing good cowboys who'd worked for me for years. It was the saddest day of my life, getting back from town, finding my vaqueros dead and my daughter taken hostage by that bastard Valdez." He glanced over to Slocum. "I'm counting on you to find Melissa for me. Do whatever it takes. Tell him I'll pay whatever he asks within reason, if that's necessary. I just can't stand the thought of losing her."

"We'll have to work out the details of getting the money to him in exchange for the girl. I'll let you know as soon as I can make contact with him," Slocum said, thinking aloud. "If we can agree on a price, then we'll also have to agree on a spot to make the trade. He'll want to stay in Mexico, that's for sure. That is liable to turn out to be the trickiest part, working it so he can't double-cross us. Once Valdez gets his hands on the money, he could have a change of heart. We need to make our trade pretty close to the border, if he's willing. When I cross over with the money, I may hire an extra pair of eyes, a man who can be trusted and someone who can use a gun if it comes down to it. No need to worry about that now, not until I find out if Valdez is interested in the proposition."

The rancher's eyes had begun to turn a little misty. "I

am only concerned with getting her back, Mr. Slocum. Working out the details will be up to you. Let me know as soon as you find out how much money he wants. I'll raise it within an hour. I only pray she's still alive . . .''

Slocum knew it was time for some brutal frankness. "You can't expect them to treat her like a lady, Mr. Anderson. I'm sure you've guessed she's been abused, if that's the right word for it. But if I can find her in time, they're more likely to stop hurting her once they know she's valuable in terms of money to them.''

"I know," Howard said hoarsely, almost a whisper, closing his eyes for a moment. "I can't bear thinking about it, but I must face the truth.''

"Time we got moving," Slocum said, rising from his chair as Tom did likewise. "If you'll pick out a gentle horse for me, one that has stamina and speed, we'll be on our way back to Laredo so I can get outfitted.''

Howard got up and offered his hand. "Good luck, Mr. Slocum. I'll be praying that you find her quickly. Let me know as soon as you know anything . . . one way or another. I'll saddle a horse and meet you around at the front.''

Slocum and Tom started for the hallway, until Howard spoke.

"One more thing. If you see her, tell her . . . that I love her with all my heart. Tell her that for me . . . that I'll be waitin' for the day when I can hold her in my arms again.''

"I'll be sure to tell her, Mr. Anderson." Slocum didn't want to add that it might not be possible to find his daughter or to free her from Valdez if he could locate her. The mountainous region around Saltillo held dozens of tiny villages and a thousand places where a bandit gang could hide. Finding Valdez would be the most troublesome part. Slocum had ridden many parts of those mountains south of Monterrey, enough to know how vast and empty they seemed to a stranger unfamiliar with the trails. And the deeper Valdez rode into the Sierra Madre Occidental, the harder he would be to find.

Tom led Slocum from the house. Outside, Tom spoke in a soft voice. ''You can see how much he's grievin', John. Hell, he'd pay everything he has to get that girl back home. He also wants revenge, but that takes a backseat to gettin' Melissa back here safe.''

Slocum cast a glance to the late morning sky. ''Revenge can be a man's downfall, Tom. Let's hope he won't do anything that might jeopardize an exchange for the girl. Keeping him away from things while a trade is being made could be real important, if I can get a deal set up. That'll be your job, making sure Howard doesn't have something up his sleeve if I can lure Valdez close to the border with his daughter.''

Tom's brow knitted. ''Howard's a hard-headed cowman. He's used to gettin' his way in Webb County, but I can make him listen to reason if he's about to do somethin' dumb.''

''Like showing up with hired guns to try to ambush Valdez as soon as his daughter is out of the way. I've got this feeling he isn't entirely giving up on his plans for vengeance. It could put the girl's life in danger.''

''And yours, besides,'' Tom added. ''I'll do my best to keep a tight rein on Howard if you can set up a trade.''

Slocum eyed Howard's expensive home, the barns and corrals. ''A rich man is more inclined to believe he's invincible, that his way of doing things is better. Wealthy men get spoiled by having their own way most of the time.''

Tom looked down at his run-over boots. ''I won't deny that he is accustomed to having things the way he wants 'em. But he's a good man inside, where it counts. He's honest. And he's damn sure worked hard for everything he owns. Don't be too hard on him, John. He's grievin' over that girl somethin' awful, which ain't all that hard to understand.''

"I understand his grief. What I want to make sure of is that it won't get in the way of a trade I might make with Valdez. It'll be hard enough to convince an outlaw like him to come close to the border. If Valdez senses that we've laid a trap for him, all hell will break loose, and I'm liable to be in the line of fire. The girl's life won't be worth a plugged nickle if Valdez thinks he's about to be bushwhacked.''

"I'll keep an eye on Howard," Tom said, keeping his voice low when the rancher came around one side of the house leading a rangy sorrel gelding.

Slocum looked the horse over carefully. Horseflesh was a commodity he knew well. The sorrel had a long under-line, deep through the heartgirth, with just the right amount of gaskin and stifle muscle. Its legs were straight, just enough bend in its hocks to make it easy-gaited, and its cannon bones were flat, of the variety Slocum preferred in his personal saddle string when he had a choice.

"Appears to have plenty of thoroughbred breeding," Slocum said offhandedly, as soon as Howard arrived at the carriage with his sorrel.

Howard grinned, albeit weakly. "This is the best of my own personal riding stock, Mr. Slocum. He's a six year old, and he can run like the wind when you put a spur to him.''

Slocum hoped he wouldn't have to find out how much bottom the sorrel had if his journey into Mexico became a horse race to reach the Rio Grande.

8

A blistering midday sun turned the streets of Laredo into a furnace. Hot wind coming from the south stirred clouds of dust from caliche roads and patches of barren earth between buildings. Dust rose in swirls, whipped by gusts of wind, forming cyclones only a few feet high whirling off into the surrounding brushland until they ended abruptly, their winds spent. Tom called them dust devils, cursing each time one swept past his porch as Slocum was packing his gear on the saddle Tom had loaned him. The blue roan gelding stood almost sixteen hands at the withers, its flanks and shoulders covered with old ranch brands. Old scars on its legs evidenced hard use in rough terrain and a few mishaps with tangled lariat ropes. But the roan was just the type of horse Slocum needed for a hard ride into the Coahuilan desert, a range-bred mate for the sorrel Howard sent along.

Slocum was dressed very differently now as he prepared for his journey toward Saltillo. He wore faded denims and a bib shirt, stovepipe boots and spurs, abandoning his city attire for clothing more suitable to blast furnace heat. He carried only a spare shirt and socks, food in the form of jerky, tortillas, and coffee. His bedroll was tied

58

behind the cantle, his war bag on a loop from the saddle horn. Saddlebags held a wide assortment of personal amenities, a razor and soap, a shard of mirror, a few medicines. The rest of his equipment could be called armament: a Winchester model 73 saddle gun in a boot below his right stirrup, a Stevens twelve gauge shotgun with barrels sawed off to twenty inches tucked inside his bedroll with its stock exposed. In his left boot, a scabbard kept a Bowie knife hidden. He wore his Colt Peacemaker and carried the little Remington belly-gun inside his shirt. The balance of weight his roan carried consisted of two canteens, a small sack of corn for his horses, and cartridges for each of his guns.

Tom inspected Slocum's preparations from the shade of his front porch without offering comment. His plump wife, Maria, was beside him. Their small house sat at the western edge of town in one of the poorer sections, proof that a city marshal's pay was a little short of what Tom might have wished for.

"That's about it," Slocum said, hanging his canteens from a pair of saddle strings below the front forks. Both horses stood hipshot in the oppressive heat, tails to the wind, heads lowered to keep dust from their eyes. "I reckon I'm as ready as I'll ever be."

Tom came to the edge of the porch. "There's a telegraph in Saltillo. Wire me if you can, or if you run into trouble. You know there ain't much I can do from here, but I'll do whatever I can."

Slocum offered his hand. "Thanks for everything, pardner. I'll send a wire if there's a need. Can't say how long I'll be gone, but I figure you'd already guessed that."

They shook. "Best of luck, John," Tom said, sounding a bit worried. "Wish the hell I could go with you. It'd be like the good old days, the two of us watchin' each other's ass."

Slocum thumbed back his hat to sleeve sweat from his forehead. ''The old days you're talking about weren't all that good, if you'll remember. Besides, I wouldn't ever want to go back to eating boiled acorns and being hungry all the time.'' He grinned. ''Don't worry none about me, Tom. I'll be okay. I make it a practice never to ride into anything I can't get myself out of in a hurry.''

A gust of wind blasted down the road in front of Tom's house as Slocum mounted his roan. Reining away from the porch, he touched the brim of his hat in a lazy salute and tickled the roan's ribs with his spurs. Leading Howard's sorrel, he rode for the river at a jog trot, tilting his hat into the wind to keep grit from his eyes. He rode backstreets, keeping away from the business district so it was less likely anyone would see him when he left town. Tom informed him that several bounty hunters who had come to Laredo seeking reward money were disgruntled when he informed them the offer had been withdrawn. Slocum wondered if one of the unhappy fortune seekers happened to be Bo Hollister. Hollister stood about as much chance of finding Melissa Anderson in this unforgiving land as he might looking for bullfrogs in a cactus patch.

Southwest of town, Slocum found a shallow crossing and sent his horses into the sluggish current. The Rio Grande was low in summer, hardly more than belly deep on his animals in the deepest spots. Spread across the south bank of the river, the city of Nuevo Laredo, mile after mile of tumbledown shacks and shanties built of adobe, rested in a broad valley ending in a desert so vast and forbidding that only men who knew its secrets ventured across it. A winding road ran due south to Monterrey, passing through tiny villages where travelers could secure water and a few necessities, occasionally decent food if a man knew where to look. Slocum had traveled this road a few times, although not in recent years, so he expected some changes.

Riding out on the south bank, he swung around the city on less traveled paths seeking the main road to Monterrey, hoping to avoid any Federale patrols that might ask questions. He carried papers of identity, but he preferred being allowed to ride past Nuevo Laredo unnoticed.

He struck the main road half an hour later and slowed his horse to a walk, saving its strength from being sapped by heat. Traveling at night, he could spare his animals and himself a measurable amount of misery. Changing horses often would allow him to cover more country, and if he avoided riding during the worst heat of the day, both geldings would be in better shape by the time he got to Saltillo.

He remembered the village of Sabinas Hidalgo between Nuevo Laredo and Monterrey, hoping he might make a few inquiries at a cantina there, to see if anyone would tell him more about Valdez and his haunts. Sometimes a piece or two of silver elicited the information he couldn't get otherwise. Money was scarce in this part of Mexico and a few silver coins spent in the right places might provide him with a scrap of news concerning Valdez since his raid across the border. If he were pressed for reasons, he meant to say he was considering the possibility of a mercenary job, if the pay was right. He wouldn't be mistaken for a Texas lawman, since everyone knew American peace officers never came across the border looking for wanted men. The American treaty with Mexico forbade that sort of thing outright, although sometimes a courageous bounty hunter slipped into the country hoping to make a payday.

Heat waves rose from the desert brush on all sides of the road, creating the illusion of distant lakes. Soon both horses were sweating and a trickle of sweat had begun down Slocum's back that quickly plastered his shirt to his skin. Mopping his brow now and then with a shirtsleeve, he continued to push down a deserted roadway crossing empty land. An occasional adobe farmhouse sat off in the brush, but for now, no one was about during the worst heat of the day to see him passing through. In the distance to the south and west, he could make out shapes of craggy mountains rising from the desert floor. The eastern edge of the Sierra Madres looked dim, far away. Suffering along with his animals, Slocum headed toward those far-off mountains at a slow pace, knowing that progress of any kind was better than none at all.

As the sun moved toward the west above him, the winds died down to a whisper. Listening to the clatter of shod hooves on sun-baked ground, Slocum passed time thinking about other things. A time or two he was distracted by rattling from a bed of cactus or a clump of brush when he rode too close. Tom's roan snorted and swung wide of the deadly sound, wise to the ways of rattlesnakes in this region where a misstep could mean twin fangs filled with poison. Here and there, horned lizards scurried away from his shadow. Again, Slocum was reminded that damn near everything in this part of the world had thorns, fangs, or razor-sharp spikes. One of the greatest hazards was a desert scorpion—its sting was sometimes fatal, for in some instances they grew to six inches in length and their venomous tails, under the best of circumstances, produced days of lingering fever and excruciating pain. Of less concern was the ponderous lizard called a gila monster, with a bite so poisonous it left men bedridden for weeks. But most dangerous of all were creatures of the two-legged variety, men with guns and bad intentions who would rob and kill travelers for the weight of their purse or the horse they rode. South of the Rio Grande, a wise man expected the worst from every situation and a pleasant surprise should things turn out otherwise.

Sunset brought a noticable cooling to the desert. Purple shadows fell away from cactus and cholla, yucca and tangles of mesquite. Spiny ocotillo plants offering no shade during the day cast curious images on the desert floor when the sun lowered. A rare tree of any size, most often an old mesquite gnarled and twisted by years of drought, sometimes appeared in the middle of a plain surrounded by clumps of brush. Mile after mile of flat sameness lay before him as dusk became dark. Although it would be cooler traveling at night, the hazards increased. Rattlesnakes fed at night, as did many other desert creatures. And in the dark, bandits often took advantage of the element of surprise when a lone traveler wasn't paying close attention to his surroundings.

Night birds whistled and chirped from dark branches in the maze of thorns blanketing the land, and always there was the clop of horseshoes beating out a rhythm accompanying his slow progress southward. Now and then he stood in his stirrups for a better look at what lay ahead, a dark thicket close to the road where an ambush might await him, or a shallow arroyo where someone could hide until he got in rifle range. The farther south he rode, the more uneasy he became.

A squat adobe building with a thatched roof sat next to the road, golden light from its paneless windows casting pale yellow squares on the adobe hardpan around it. Six rawboned horses were tied to hitching posts at the front. They bore open-tree saddles typical of those ridden by Mexican vaqueros. A pair of burros harnessed to a two-wheeled cart stood behind the adobe. Slocum took note of the horses and decided to ride past the cantina in hopes of avoiding any trouble with tequila-fueled cowboys, as he counted the horses again, figuring the odds. At least six men were inside the little cantina, and someone was there who drove the burro cart. The six could be simple cowboys having a drink after a hard day in the saddle. Or they could be highwaymen on the lookout for easy pickings, a lone traveler they could rob. A drink of whiskey or tequila, even a gourd dipper of pulque or a lukewarm glass of green Mexican beer would have seemed nice after a half day's ride through this miserable heat and dust. But in order to cut the trail dust from his throat, Slocum would have to take a chance that the men inside were friendly. It wasn't his nature to let others crowd him away from things he wanted, but a young girl's life might be hanging in the balance and should any misfortune prevent him from meeting with Victoriano Valdez to try to arrange for Melissa Anderson's release, the girl might suffer longer needlessly. Thus he made up his mind to ride past the cantina despite a powerful thirst for distilled spirits. He had whiskey in his saddlebags, anyway.

As he was trotting his horses past the front of the building, two men wearing sombreros came to the doorway to stare at him. He touched his hat brim and continued on down the two-rut road without slowing his horses' gait. He noticed that neither of the vaqueros were wearing gun belts.

''Probably just cowboys,'' he told himself quietly, glancing over his shoulder once, making sure no one meant to follow him.

The cantina fell away behind him until he could barely make out light from the windows. Reaching into one of his saddlebags, he took out a fresh pint of sour mash whiskey and pulled its cork with his teeth. He drank deeply, sighing, enjoying the subtle burn of good spirits sliding down his throat. It required only a slight tug on his reins to slow the road-weary roan to a walk, so as not to spill a precious drop of whiskey.

"That's better," he said aloud, after taking another swallow of corn squeeze, as it was called when he was a boy back in his native Georgia. Calhoun County was known across the state for its home-brewed whiskey, some of the best anywhere. His father had been a publicly religious man who disclaimed having a liking for liquor, calling it the devil's brew. But in private, William Slocum kept jars of whiskey hidden in the barn and on more than one occasion, John found his father kneeling behind a hay mow with a jar of the devil's mixture held to his lips.

Slocum drank again and returned the cork to the neck of his pint, after a warm feeling began to spread from the pit of his stomach to other parts of his body. He was somewhat hungry now and at the next opportunity, when he found a piece of ground high enough to allow him to see in every direction, he meant to stop long enough to chew jerky and eat a couple of Maria's tortillas. His horses needed water and a handful of corn, yet finding water presented a problem of major proportions. There had been a water trough behind the cantina, but the risks of stopping he felt were too great, outnumbered by at least six or seven to one. If he remembered the road correctly, Sabinas Hidalgo was only a few hours farther south. There, he expected to be able to find water and fewer risks of any problems with roving bandits, for Sabinas was large enough to support a small Federale garrison, keeping lawless desperados in check merely by their presence.

As he was putting his whiskey back in his saddlebags, he took a look down his back trail, and what he saw brought him up short, straightening in the saddle. A group of horsemen was following him. He could see their pale

dust rising from the road even in light from a sprinkling
of stars.

"Trouble coming," he muttered, reaching for his Winchester.

9

Slocum kept his horses in a steady lope toward the lip of a shallow ravine where the road made a bend, certain that the men behind him were from the cantina and that they were bent on ill purpose. Sighting over his shoulder, he could make out the dim outlines of riders coming for him at a gallop. A gunfight was in the offing, a battle over his horses and saddles and what gold and silver he carried in his poke. Depending upon how well his pursuers were armed and how desperate they were, he could be in for the most one-sided fight of his life.

He reined over the top of the ravine and felt his roan make a plunge to the bottom. The arroyo was scarcely six feet deep, but it would be enough to provide cover from flying lead. As he swung down from the saddle, he fashioned a loop in one rein and tied it to a branch of a nearby mesquite bush before scrambling to the top of the cutbank with his rifle. Levering a cartridge into the firing chamber, he peered over the rim just as six men spurred lathered horses toward the arroyo at full speed, manes and tails of their horses flying in the wind. He could hear the clank of spur rowels drumming against the horses' sides above the rumble of drumming hooves. With two hundred yards between him and the Mexicans he rested his rifle sights on one rider at the front, waiting, aiming high for the cone-shaped crown of his sombrero.

"I'll warn him first," Slocum snarled, feeling the beat of his heart quicken as danger came near. He curled his finger on the trigger gently, a nudge that would not ruin his aim.

His Winchester roared, slamming into his shoulder. A ball of molten lead belched from the muzzle amid the clap of exploding gunpowder. A stabbing finger of bright light spat forth from the top of the ravine, and an instant later there was a distant cry when a sombrero rose skyward, spinning like a child's top above a rider's head. Riders swerved off the road in confusion, trying to rein plunging, frightened horses into the safety of the brush on either side of the roadway. Shouts echoed through the night as men called out to each other.

Two quick gunshots answered Slocum's rifle blast, the pop of pistols. Somewhere high above Slocum's head a slug whistled away harmlessly toward the stars.

Performing mechanically, a practiced motion, Slocum levered another shell into the firing chamber, paying no heed to an empty brass cartridge casing tinkling musically to the ground near his feet. Behind him, the blue roan snorted over the explosion and pawed the ground, although the noise did not interfere with his concentration when Slocum sought another target among the dark shadows milling about in the brushland. Riders charged in every direction into the tangled thorns and cactus, hoping to escape the next shot fired from the arroyo. One horseman toppled from his saddle when his horse stumbled over something hidden in the darkness. Slocum heard the man yell when he landed, cursing in Spanish, apparently unharmed despite being unseated from a horse running at full speed before it fell.

"*Donde esta?*" someone cried, asking where the rifleman was. Slocum spoke only a few words of Spanish, yet he understood the simple question readily enough.

The drum of hoofbeats faded, moving farther away.

"Maybe I scared 'em off," he whispered, scanning every foot of terrain before him, keeping his rifle to his shoulder.

A riderless horse wandered off, trotting back down the road in the direction from which it came. Hidden somewhere in a mass of thorny limbs was the Mexican who had fallen off. Slocum had to keep an eye open for a man afoot now, as well as watch for the return of the riders.

West of the road, three horsemen came together to talk over what to do next. One was hatless, the man who had ridden at the front when Slocum took aim at a sombrero. For a short time they sat their horses a quarter mile away, obviously discussing what had happened. Then one reined his mount for the wagon road and took off at a trot, heading back toward the cantina. A moment later, the other two followed, casting wary looks at the ravine from time to time until they rode out of sight.

"Leaves three more," Slocum muttered. In the darkness and confusion, he'd lost track of the men who scattered into the brush on the east side of the roadway. Two were mounted, a third left on foot now that his horse had wandered off. It was boiling down to a waiting game to see if the others rushed him.

Sweat trickled down his back and down his face from his hat band while he waited, watching closely for any sign of movement in the brush. His ears were still ringing from the rifle explosion so close to his face and for that reason he couldn't quite trust his hearing. Cocking his head this way and that, he listened carefully for any strange sound, the slightest noise, as his gaze wandered back and forth across the dark landscape.

Then he saw them, two riders crossing a gentle swell in the prairie almost a mile away, backgrounded by night sky made bright by winking stars. The pair was leaving their horseless companion to fend for himself.

"Can't say your pardners turned out to be very good friends in a tight spot," he said quietly, addressing the unfortunate man who had lost his seat, though Slocum said it to himself in a soft voice only he could hear. But without knowing whether the Mexican was armed, it was a fool's move to ride out of the ravine until he knew the last Mexican's whereabouts. For the present, it had become a stalemate of sorts, neither man willing to make the first attempt to withdraw from the scene or continue the fight.

I'll have to wait him out, Slocum thought, relaxing his grip on the stock of his rifle somewhat. Backing away from the rim, he walked quietly to his saddlebags and took out the pint bottle for a quick pull, to help steady his nerves. Even though the gunfight had been short, and only three shots had been fired, it had been enough to rattle him a little.

Then he heard it, a distant wail in Spanish, a voice so thin he had trouble hearing it: "*Por favor, señor!*"

Slocum hurried back to the edge of the cutbank, peering over it cautiously. He saw a man standing a hundred yards away with arms raised over his head. Covering the Mexican with his rifle, he waited, puzzling over the voice.

"*Por favor, señor!* Do not shoot me!"

Now the man spoke a mixture of Spanish and English. Both of his hands were empty. "Come over here!" Slocum shouted. "Keep those hands where I can see them!"

Slowly, one hesitant footstep at a time, the Mexican began to walk toward the arroyo with his palms held high.

"Please do not shoot me, señor!" he called again. "I have no gun!"

"Keep walking! I won't shoot so long as I can see that your hands are empty!"

Dodging thicker clumps of thorny plants, the Mexican continued forward, his spurs making a clanking sound when he struck a stretch of bare ground. Listening to the man's voice, he sounded young, hardly much more than a boy. The closer he got, the more Slocum was convinced there was no harm in him now. He was skinny and short, slightly bowlegged, not threatening in appearance, and he seemed to be unarmed.

Slocum waited until the Mexican was ten yards away before he rose above the lip of the ravine to show himself, keeping his gun muzzle on the man's chest. "Keep coming," he said, motioning with his rifle barrel.

A boy walked up to Slocum, his face showing fear. He held his hands aloft, albeit they trembled greatly while he held them above his head.

"Why'd you and your pardners come after me like that?" he asked, lowering his Winchester when it was plain the boy wasn't concealing a gun.

The Mexican swallowed hard. "My compadres were very drunk, señor. They wanted to take your money and your caballos. But when you shot off Diego's sombrero, we were all very much afraid of you. My caballo fell in a gopher hole and I lost my *pistola* in the dark. Please do not kill me, señor, for I am not a bad man in my heart. It was too much tequila that made us do this thing to you."

"I believe you. Tell me your name."

"I am Ramón Casillas. I am a vaquero for Rancho Bustamante. I am not a bad man, I swear it before *Dios!* I drank too much of the tequila tonight and I listened to bad amigos who wanted to do a robbery. For this, señor,

I am very sorry. I pray you will not kill me for making this big mistake.''

"I won't kill you, Ramón. You can put your hands down.''

"*Gracias, señor,*" he said, lowering his arms to his sides.

Slocum wondered what to do with the boy. He had no horse and his friends had abandoned him as soon as the shooting began.

"How far do you have to walk to get to this ranch where you work?''

"Many hours, señor. Rancho Bustamante is near the village of Sabinas Hidalgo.''

Hearing the boy's story, Slocum found himself feeling a bit sorry for the kid. "I'm headed that way. I reckon I could let you ride my spare horse most of the way, so long as you act real peaceable about it and don't try to run off.''

"I would be very grateful, señor. It is most kind of you to make such an offer to a bandit who was planning to rob you. I have only a little money, a few pesos, but I will gladly pay for the use of your spare horse.''

"That won't be necessary. An apology will do. Just make damn sure you don't have a gun hidden underneath your shirt. I'd hate like hell to have to kill you.''

To show he had no weapon, Ramón pulled his home-spun cotton shirt from his pants and turned around, revealing how thin he was under his clothing, bony ribs jutting through thin hide. "I have no gun, señor. I owned an old *pistola,* but when my horse tripped, I dropped it in the dark and now I cannot find it. I give you my word I will not try to steal your horse, if only you will allow me to ride it to Sabinas Hidalgo.''

"Come on over," Slocum said quietly, balancing his Winchester in his left palm. "You ain't much of a robber and neither are your amigos. They sure as hell ran off and left you the minute a slug got too close to 'em.''

"It was the tequila," Ramón said again, walking hesitantly to the lip of the arroyo, grinning sheepishly. "We have never robbed anyone before. It was Diego's idea, when he saw a lone gringo riding past Arturo's cantina. Arturo warned against it, but Diego would not listen. I did not listen, señor, and for this I am truly sorry."

"You've apologized enough," Slocum said, inclining his head toward the sorrel. "Mount up on that red gelding, and we'll be on our way to Sabinas." It was then that a thought occurred to him. Perhaps the boy knew something about Victoriano Valdez. "I'm on my way to Saltillo, trying to locate a revolutionary leader who is called Victoriano. I have a business proposition for him if he'll listen."

Ramón stopped short, looking into Slocum's face. "You are seeking the great general, Victoriano Valdez?"

"That's him. I've got some money for him if he has what I'm looking for."

At that, Ramón stood a little straighter. "My cousin Pedro Morales rides with General Valdez, señor. I can take you to the general's camp, but I must warn you that it will be very dangerous. The general has sworn to kill anyone who betrays his hiding place to the Federales."

"I'm not a Federale. I've got a business deal for Valdez if he's interested in making some money. A revolutionary army needs money for guns and ammunition. Maybe General Valdez would like to hear what I've got to offer."

Ramón appeared to hesitate. "Maybeso I could ride there to tell my cousin about your offer. Pedro can decide if the general will listen to what you have to say."

"That'll be better than nothing, Ramón. You can make a few dollars in American silver by helping me out."

"How much silver, señor?"

Slocum thought it over, considering the risks the boy would be taking. "Twenty dollars, after you take my message to Valdez."

The boy grinned. "For twenty dollars I will take you to see *El Diablo* himself, señor."

Walking over to the roan, Slocum booted his rifle and untied his reins. "Mount up," he said, sticking his toe in the stirrup, and pulling himself into the saddle. As soon as he was on the roan, he gave the boy the sorrel's lead rope. "Put a bridle on him and let's get started. Remember, I'm carrying a Colt .44, and if you try anything funny, I'll put a bullet in you before you can get fifty feet away. The only way you'll live long enough to collect that twenty dollars is by doing exactly what you promised to do, taking me to Valdez. Anything short of that will get you killed."

"I swear it, señor. The only thing I ask is that we stop at the rancho to tell Señor Bustamante I will be visiting my cousin. That way he will know where I am and that I will return to work as soon as I have contacted Pedro."

"Just so long as it ain't too far out of the way. The offer I have for Valdez depends upon nothing happening to an American girl he has with him. If any harm has come to her, the deal's off."

Even in the dark Slocum could tell Ramón was frowning. "Why does the general have this American girl with him, señor?"

Slocum gave a measured reply. "Seems he may have taken her against her will. The girl's father wants her back and he's more than willing to pay to get her out of Mexico. This is what I want you to tell your cousin, that I'm bringing a handsome offer for the girl's safe return to the border."

They rode out of the ravine at a walk, heading south.

10

Melissa stared vacantly out a window overlooking a walled courtyard, numbed almost to the point of unconsciousness. The bitter tasting medicine they gave her always made her so sleepy and sometimes, when they gave it too often, her arms and legs refused to work properly. It was when Victoriano came to see her that she was forced to drink the medicine. She had been told it was for the bleeding coming from inside her after Victoriano had his way with her that first night. But the bleeding had stopped days ago and yet she was still being forced to take swallows of tonic.

Despite her sleepy condition, there were several things she was grateful for. Victoriano no longer required that she be tied to the bed when he used her, and when his prick entered her so deeply it did not hurt as much as it used to. They also allowed her freedom within this upstairs room overlooking a courtyard and a pretty fountain. She knew they were in a mountain village somewhere in Mexico. She remembered being tied to the back of a horse again and escorted by armed guards along a high mountain trail to a walled village. The nights were cold and days were hot, like today. On mountain slopes above the city she could see herds of goats grazing, being tended by small Mexican boys and dogs. The food they gave her was good, roasted quail or goat meat seasoned with chilis, sometimes a piece of beefsteak. And she noticed a subtle change in Victoriano lately. He was not as rough with her when he took her. Sometimes he could almost be gentle when his cock was inside her, unless he was drunk, which happened quite often.

She was given pretty dresses to wear made by women in the village, brightly colored gowns woven from spun cotton and wool dyed different shades with Indian designs on them. Every morning a Mexican woman brought buckets of steaming water to her room so she could bathe in a cast iron tub behind a dressing screen in a corner of the room. The woman, whose name was Consuelo, combed her hair for her and washed her clothes somewhere downstairs. A guard stood outside her door preventing her from leaving, but for the most part she was being treated well . . . until Victoriano came to her room.

Victoriano was a crude, insensitive brute who had no respect for her. The times he treated her gently were few, and even then he made her feel dirty, unclean, when he lay on top of her with his prick moving in and out of her. Sometimes he grinned at her with his horrible gold tooth gleaming in his mouth and Melissa could have sworn he was a likeness of the devil, what scripture said the devil looked like, if only he had horns jutting from his head. There was a wickedness about him, a countenance that was decidedly evil. His breath was always foul and he was often dirty when he came to her room, reeking of sweat. He was the most repugnant man she could ever have imagined, and it was with him that she first experienced what it was like to be entered by a man's cock.

Slowly, the sleepy feeling was ebbing away. Last night he had come to her room, forcing her to drink more medicine before he took off her clothes and pushed her down on the bed. She no longer made any real effort to fend him off, since it was useless to resist. He was much too powerful to deny him what he wanted and when she had tried, in the beginning, he hit her so hard that her face remained swollen for days. Most of her bruises were healed by now, but not the scars across her soul left by the dark knowledge that he had taken away her virginity. She was a fallen woman now, what some men called a soiled dove. No man would ever want her, not after what Victoriano had done. Even her best and dearest boyfriend, Danny Rogers, would spurn her when he learned she was not a virgin. A blacker thought was that she might not ever see Danny again, or her father, or the ranch beside the Rio Grande she loved so much. It was quite possible that Victoriano would keep her a prisoner forever, or until he grew tired of her, and then he might decide to kill her when he was finished using her. At night she prayed that she would not get pregnant by him and have his baby. It would be a fate worse than death to bear a child fathered by such a horrible beast.

She knew her father would be beside himself with worry and grief. If there were any way to send help, he would do so. But Melissa had lived on the Mexican border long enough to know that the laws in Texas were meaningless here, and that no lawmen from the United States could enter Mexico to help her. Howard would come himself if he could, if he knew how to handle this sort of thing. But her father was a peaceful man and he wasn't skilled with a gun. Someone would have to rescue her who was a capable fighter, and judging by the size of the army Victoriano had, it would require a force of equal strength to set her free.

Overwhelmed by so many dark thoughts, Melissa continued to stare out her window sadly, wondering if she would ever see her father again, or Danny, or any of the ranch hands. She recalled that many of them had been shot during the terrible attack on the ranch, lying dead or wounded in the ranch yard as she was being taken from the house by two of Victoriano's men. She had seen a favorite ranch hand, Carlos Lopez, lying in a flower garden with blood pouring from a hole in his stomach. She remembered screaming for her father that day, although he had been in Laredo on ranch business. It was the worst day of her life, and she knew she would never forget it as long as she lived.

Watching the small fountain at the center of the courtyard, she let her mind wander, seeking more pleasant memories as if they might help shut out the horror of what had happened.

Heavy boots sounded on the stairs. Melissa recognized that sound and she shuddered. Victoriano was coming for her. Steeling herself for what what would take place, she sat on the edge of her bed and waited for the door to open. In spite of a wish not to, she felt tears forming in the corners of her eyes. She was too old to cry, she told herself.

Glancing out her bedroom window, she discovered it was dark. Somehow an entire day had passed without her realizing it. She knew it had to be the medicine they gave her that was making her too drowsy to be aware of the passage of time.

A key entered the lock. Her door swung inward. Filling the doorway with his massive shoulders, Victoriano stood for a moment looking at her across the room, his gold tooth gleaming in light from the lamp on the bedside table. Melissa saw the familiar lavender bottle in his hand.

"No more medicine, please!" she begged softly, as more tears came to her eyes.

Victoriano grunted. "It is not for you to decide, *mi*

hita.'' He came into the room slowly and closed the heavy oak door behind him. A guard's boots shuffled over in front of the door, blocking anyone else from entering. Victoriano glanced down at the front of Melissa's red cotton dress where it was open, revealing only the tops of her small, firm breasts. "Take it off," he snapped. "Then take a swallow of this laudanum. It will make you feel so much better. The doctor has promised it will make you well."

"But I'm not sick," she protested, "and it makes me feel so sleepy."

Victoriano's face twisted to a scowl. "Take it, *mi hita,* or I will pour it down your pretty throat." He came across the floor and took a cork from the neck of the bottle, glaring down at her with the blackest eyes she had ever seen.

She took the bottle and drank a small swallow.

"More," he insisted, the threat in his voice unmistakable in the silence of her room.

She drank again, making a face when its bitter taste made her pucker.

He took the bottle and corked it, placing it beside the lamp. "Now take off the dress, pretty one. Show me what your body looks like tonight. Every night I must be reminded of how perfect you are. Take the dress off slowly and drop it on the floor around your ankles."

She got up, feeling slightly dizzy the way she always did after taking laudanum, although sometimes the feeling was pleasant. Unfastening a cord binding the front of her gown, she let the ends fall loosely and wriggled her dress off her shoulders. She was naked underneath her gown, and when Victoriano saw her pubic mound, the scowl left his face.

"Turn around," he said huskily, his eyes roaming up to the swell of her breasts, her hardening nipples. "I like to look at your ass, my yellow-haired beauty. You have a nice ass, so soft and so round.''

Melissa turned, noticing that her dizziness had increased to a point that she feared she might fall. ''The medicine,'' she said in a slightly fuzzy voice.

Suddenly her knees gave way. She fell across the bed on her chest, her mind swimming. A moment later she felt a hand cup one cheek of her buttocks. The mattress quivered when Victoriano put his tremendous weight on it. Melissa felt him spread her legs as he came between them. Then the head of his cock touched her cunt and she winced.

He entered her, only the head of his thick prick stretching the lips of her cunt wide. A glimmer of pain flashed through her groin and she groaned in protest, ''Don't hurt me, please . . .''

Victoriano laughed, a cruel laugh telling her how much he enjoyed hurting her this way.

''It will not hurt in a moment, *mi hita*, when your juices are making your pussy wet.''

''It hurts,'' she said, the words slurred by laudanum and with her mouth pressed to the bedcovers.

He pushed more cock into her, another inch, grunting when he did so.

Melissa closed her eyes, fighting back a rush of hot tears flooding her cheeks. She knew she could endure the pain, as she had so many times since they took her from the ranch. It was not only the pain bringing tears to her eyes, but the humiliation.

''Now it will feel good,'' Victoriano promised, as he began to make short thrusts into her cunt, driving his cock deeper.

But there was more pain each time he pushed his stiff prick farther inside her, rocking the mattress with the power of his thrusts. Gritting her teeth, Melissa dug her fingernails into the bedspread, preparing herself for more hurt. It was slightly more painful when he took her from behind, the way he was now, yet it did no good to protest this position.

The bed rocked and swayed as he drove farther up her cunt, until at last the hilt of his shaft was buried between the lips of her pussy. His prick throbbed with desire while his heavy hips drew his cock back and forth.

Soon she was gasping for air, panting, and as it had in the past on a few occasions, accompanying the hurt was a warm feeling that was part good, part pain. Victoriano's thrusts grew faster now as he neared a climax. With her eyelids tightly closed, she whispered to herself that soon it would be over.

He had been resting his weight on his elbows, when suddenly he fell across her back while hunching furiously to achieve his orgasm. His balls exploded and he let out a muffled yelp as his climax came.

Warm, wet seed spewed from his prick into her cunt and she gasped, barely able to breathe with his weight pressing her to the mattress. "Please get off!" she cried, the sound stifled by lack of air.

He thrust once more and grunted, sweat from his hairy chest wetting her back and shoulders.

"Please get off—you're too heavy!" she begged.

At last he lifted himself with his palms, his stale breath brushing her cheek when he said, "That was good, my pretty one."

Finally able to breathe again, she merely nodded, keeping her eyes tightly closed.

"Did you like it?" he asked, a hint of demand in the tone he used.

When she did not answer him immediately, he delivered a stinging blow with an open palm across her face.

She cried out and drew away, watching him now to see if he meant to hit her again.

"Did you like it?" he shouted, filling the bedroom with the boom of his voice.

"Yes," she whimpered softly, humiliated and at the same time afraid he would strike her again if she refused to tell him what he wanted to hear.

He withdrew his softening cock from her and got off the bed to fasten the front of his pants. "Answer me the first time I ask you a question, *puta*!"

She could scarcely manage a nod with her mind afloat in the effects of laudanum, although she did so to keep from being hit. She felt his jism wetting the bed between her thighs as it dribbled out of her, and she mouthed a silent prayer that there would be no baby forming inside her.

To stem another tide of tears, she thought about the ranch, a favorite swimming hole in a creek along the northwest boundary of a winter pasture where she swam in summer without her clothes. Sometimes she swam her chestnut pony into the creek so she could dive off its back. The swimming hole had been her own secret hideaway since she was old enough to ride there on her own. She only told her father about it when he asked why her hair was wet one summer day after she got home. It would be so nice, she thought, to be swimming in that deep pool of water today, rather than being held prisoner by a monster who used her so heartlessly.

11

Ramón rode beside Slocum across a prairie brightening with sunrise. The road to Sabinas Hidalgo ran arrow-straight through mile after mile of thorny undergrowth and scattered stands of mesquite trees. As dawn came, they passed occasional burro carts laden with woven baskets, clay pottery, sometimes bushel bags of corn. Now and then a few vaqueros rode in small bunches toward another day's labor gathering wild longhorn cattle from land so impossibly dry and rugged that Slocum found it hard to believe animals could exist on it. From time to time they glimpsed a few longhorns moving through tangles of mesquite, nibbling on beans growing from low branches. Mesquite beans were the only edible things in this waste-land, Slocum decided, besides a few clumps of dry bunch-grass hidden below a thorny limb or yucca spines.

Ramón talked freely now, apparently convinced Slo-cum wasn't going to kill him for his role in the attempted robbery. The boy told him several things about Victoriano Valdez that might come in handy. Valdez, calling himself a general, recruited men from mountain villages across Tamaulipas and Coahuila to overthrow the government in Mexico City in order to give back farmland to the poor.

Valdez plundered rich ranches, sharing some of the spoils with poor people, making him something of a legend among simple peons who worked for wealthy landowners. Ramón's cousin, Pedro, believed in Valdez's cause and joined his revolutionary army last year. Of late, however, Pedro began telling Ramón he'd become disillusioned with the general's promises. Valdez wasn't fighting Federales or making any attempt to topple the government in Mexico City. Instead, he continued to raid and loot ranches and larger farms for the booty, keeping most for himself. Men who rode with Valdez were beginning to grumble that their leader did not believe in patriotism after all, that he merely used a cause as an excuse for banditry. Slocum wondered how widespread this low morale was. Could it be a weak link that might allow him to get close to the girl?

Ramón pointed to an offshoot trail east of the road. "This is the way to Rancho Bustamante, señor. It is only a few miles to the rancho. I will tell Señor Bustamante that I must visit my cousin for a short time. We can water these caballos there and be on our way *muy pronto*."

Slocum nodded, following the boy eastward when they came to a pair of dim ruts. Ramón didn't seem like a bad kid, only that he occasionally listened to bad advice from his friends. During the night, the boy told him what it was like working on a cattle ranch in this unforgiving land. Water was as precious as gold to cowmen here, and during a drought, cattle died by the score when wells dried up, or from starvation when there was no grass and a poor crop of mesquite beans. Life for a cowboy was equally tough when it did not rain. Men suffered along with animals when the corn crop came in short. Ramón recalled several years when there was hardly any food for his family. Being poor, going to bed hungry night after night, was one reason men listened to promises made by Victoriano Valdez. Valdez told them a new government was needed, to see that poor families got enough to eat. The idea had broad appeal among men who were very hungry.

"How close is General Valdez's hideout to Saltillo?" Slocum asked.

"Not far," Ramón replied, a bit nervous about the question. "I cannot take you there, but I will go myself to visit Pedro. I will inform the general that you wish to see him about the matter concerning this girl, but I would be killed if I took you there."

"I understand. I was only wondering how far you'd have to ride to get there."

"Half a day's ride, señor, into the mountains. That is all I should tell you. Several times each year the general moves to another village. *Por favor*, do not ask me to say any more."

Slocum let the subject drop. Half a day's ride in mountain country was probably only fifteen or twenty miles. Valdez relied upon fear to keep his hiding place a secret. Shooting anyone who gave his location away was motivation enough to keep most wagging tongues still.

Crossing a gentle rise in the brushland, they came in sight of a ranch house and several pole corrals. The house was small by most comparisons, made of adobe mud with a clay tile roof and a long porch across the front. The corrals held a few horses, a smaller number of burros, and a handful of thin longhorn cows in a corral by themselves.

"Rancho Bustamante," Ramón said. "Do not worry. You will be welcome here."

They heeled the horses to a trot, angling toward a windmill where a water trough sat beneath it. Both horses scented water, and they had no trouble holding them at a steady pace. A white dog began to bark at their approach from a shady spot on the porch. At the sound of the dog, a man came out of the adobe to shade his eyes from a rising sun to see who was coming.

Ramón turned in the saddle. "I would ask one small favor of you, señor. Please do not tell Señor Bustamante about what I did last night. Señor Bustamante is an honest man, and if he knew I was trying to rob someone, he would send me away."

"We'll keep it between the two of us," Slocum agreed, more than ever believing Ramón had been the victim of bad companions when he joined his friends in the robbery attempt.

They rode to the front of the house. An aging Mexican with a handlebar mustache nodded to Ramón, then to Slocum.

"*Buenos días*," the old man said, his gaze wandering to the guns Slocum carried.

Ramón jumped to the ground. "Señor Bustamante, this is my friend, Señor John Slocum. I must ask that you let me go to see my cousin, Pedro, so that Señor Slocum might be able to do some business with him."

Bustamante frowned at the boy. "Does this business have to do with Victoriano?" he asked sharply.

Slocum interrupted before Ramón could reply. "It has to do with money being offered for the return of an American girl who may be a prisoner of Valdez. All I want to know is if the girl is with them. Ramón will not be involved. As soon as he has contacted his cousin, he will be heading back here. There won't be any danger for the boy."

Bustamante listened, but he still seemed doubtful. "It is very bad for this boy to go there. Victoriano makes these young men bold promises, yet he does little to keep his word to them. I do not want Ramón to hear these false promises about revolution." He stared into Ramón's face. "Do not listen to Victoriano. From his lips only come terrible lies."

"*Sí*, Señor Bustamante. I will not listen, I will only ask Pedro to inquire of the general about a meeting with Señor John Slocum. That is all."

"Very well, then, you may go. Come back quickly, for there is much work to be done here."

"May we water the horses?" Ramón asked.

"Of course," Bustamante said, pointing to the trough. "It is common courtesy that any traveler may share what water we have here. Let the horses drink, and fill your canteens."

"I'm obliged," Slocum said, touching his hat brim. "I'll be sure to have the boy headed back this way as soon as I can. I aim to pay him for his trouble."

When Bustamante looked at Slocum's horses, his frown returned. He spoke to Ramón. "Where is the *bayo* caballo?"

Ramón blushed and looked at his feet. "The horse tripped in a gopher hole last night. I fell off and the *bayo* ran away. My amigo Diego will find it and keep it for me until I return. It was a foolish thing, Señor Bustamante."

"Is the *caballo* injured?" Bustamante asked.

"No, señor. It ran away like the wind. I walked to the camp of Señor Slocum, and he offered to let me ride this sorrel to *el rancho*."

The old man seemed satisfied. "Take another caballo from the corral. You must have one to ride back from Saltillo when your business with Pedro is finished. But remember what I told you about listening to Victoriano's promises. He is nothing but a bandido who calls himself a general."

Ramón led the sorrel over to the water trough and handed the reins to Slocum. "I will saddle another caballo and be ready to ride *en uno momentito, señor*."

Slocum swung down, weary after a night without sleep. He let the horses drink their fill while he was filling one of the canteens, noticing that Señor Bustamante was talking to Ramón at the corrals as the boy was saddling a dappled gray mustang. It was easy to guess the old man was lecturing Ramón about losing his bay horse last night.

Slocum passed a glance around the small ranch. It was spare and primitive in appearance, hardly the sort of cattle ranch one found north of the border. Life was hard for farmers and ranchers in this waterless part of Mexico. Livestock barely managed to exist on what little grazing there was. Cattle in the corral were mostly hide and bones and horns. He wondered how the old man showed a profit here from year to year.

Ramón came trotting from a small saddle shed leading his gray pony. By the color showing in his cheeks, he was smarting from the lecture Señor Bustamante gave him. When he arrived at the water trough, he looked over his shoulder.

"Señor Bustamante is very angry at me," he said. "He told me I should not have come back without the caballo. I did not tell him the truth about how I fell. He warned me to come back in three days or I will not have a job at the rancho."

Slocum did not say that it didn't appear to be much of a job in the first place. He wondered idly what the boy was paid. "Let's get moving," he said, mounting wearily, feeling sleepy. "If we push, we can make Saltillo by late tonight, if we don't run into any trouble."

Ramón swung aboard his gray mustang and reined for the road to Monterrey, tugging his sombrero down over his eyes to keep out the sun. Slocum turned back and waved to Señor Bustamante, who was watching them from the shade of a livestock shed. The old man returned his wave and went into the barn as they took off at an easy jog trot.

Turning south on the Monterrey road, they encountered

more wagon traffic and travelers. Dust rose from the wheels of big freight wagons drawn by oxen or spans of mules. Teamsters' whips cracked above the backs of laboring animals. Above them a clear sky warned of another hot day as the sun climbed. They held their horses in a trot for half an hour, then slowed to a walk when heat brought sweat to the horses' coats. In places the road had turned to chalky powder where wagon wheels ground caliche to dust. Choking clouds of alkali hovered above the wagons and carts as they crept in both directions along what had become a very heavily traveled roadway. Slocum remembered Monterrey as being a sizable city, which explained much heavier wagon traffic heading to and from the town. Last night they'd had the road pretty much to themselves.

An hour later, they rode through Sabinas Hidalgo, hardly more than a water stop for thirsty teams and saddle horses crossing the Tamaulipas desert. A few dusty stores and shops advertised their wares with faded signs above windows and doors.

"If there's a good place to eat here, we'll stop for a bite," Slocum suggested.

Ramón pointed to a tiny adobe building at the south edge of town. "Manuel sells the best cabrito in all the world, señor. It is very spicy and we will need plenty of water, but the goat meat is good."

Slocum swung his horse over to a rail in front of Manuel's and got down. He handed Ramón a few pieces of silver. "Buy us a handful of meat and some tortillas. We'll eat in the shade of that big tree yonder. It's close to the well, so we can cool off our tongues if the need arises."

Ramón laughed. "A Mexican will not need water, señor, but I think it would be wise for a gringo to fill Manuel's bucket, if you are not used to chilis and serranos."

The boy ran inside, sensing that Slocum wanted to avoid any unnecessary delay. While Ramón was buying goat meat, Slocum led their animals over to a towering live oak tree providing shade over the stone and mortar lip around a well. He sent down a wood bucket on a piece of sisal rope, wondering how much longer he could go without a few hours of sleep. Already this difficult journey into the desert was telling on him.

Ramón hurried over with a piece of butcher paper wrapped around slices of delicious-smelling cabrito. Warm flour tortillas rested on top of the pile.

Slocum took a tortilla, noticing a thick layer of red pepper on each strip of meat, hoping he wouldn't regret having eaten a variety of food his stomach was not accustomed to. But when he bit into a sandwich of tortilla and cabrito, he was rewarded with a taste far better than he imagined. "It's mighty good," he told the boy, chewing contentedly.

It was half a minute later before the red pepper did its work on Slocum's tongue and mouth, sending him quickly to the bucket for a dipper of cool water. "That's hot enough to melt down a horseshoe," he said, after several swallows.

Ramón laughed heartily, still eating without having taken a drink. "In Mexico you must like peppers," he said, grinning with a mouthful of food in his cheeks. "Otherwise, señor, you will starve to death here."

They ate quickly and climbed back into their saddles. Slocum wanted to arrive in Saltillo before midnight, before he fell off his horse sound asleep.

12

Saltillo had once been held by the French during colonization efforts from Europe. An imposing French fortress sat on a mountainside overlooking a valley where the village was built, yet there were also many signs of early Spanish colonization: a few large churches with tall bell towers and very old haciendas with walled courtyards. Tonight the town was quiet when Slocum and Ramón rode in. A number of lamplit cantinas sounded of guitar music and laughter, but most windows were dark. An old cut stone and adobe hotel sat across from a big central plaza, looking like it offered spacious rooms. Slocum chose this place to spend the night. He was bone tired and stiff from too many hours in the saddle. When he got down off the sorrel gelding's back, he tested his aching legs to make sure they would support his weight.

"See if you can find a livery for these horses," he told the boy, taking down his bedroll and the rest of his gear, including his rifle. "I'll hire us a room. Make sure our animals get the best care, grain and hay. Don't worry about how much it costs."

He gave Ramón a few silver coins, hoisted his war bag and guns for a slow climb up a set of stone steps to the front door. As Ramón led their horses away, Slocum stepped inside the hotel, too weary to think of anything beyond a clean bed and a few hours of badly needed shut-eye.

Dawn came late to this mountain valley, the sun shielded to the east by wooded peaks. Forests of stunted pine, which Ramón called piñon, clung to steep slopes around Saltillo, and a deep green blanket of grass grew between stands of trees. They ate a breakfast of chorizo sausages and eggs with warm tortillas before the sun appeared over the mountains, taking their meal at a tiny street corner café across the plaza from the hotel. Slocum felt truly rested for the first time in days. The people of Saltillo were out early herding goats down narrow roadways toward slopes thick with grass, buying food at a market west of the plaza, some driving burro carts loaded with all manner of wares. Slocum was paying particular attention to a troop of mounted Federales near a gate into the ancient French fortress.

"Where do you reckon those soldiers are headed?" he asked, wondering if Ramón knew anything about Federale patrols in the region.

The boy's cheeks were stuffed with food. He swallowed and pointed south. "They will ride the main roads, señor. It is a show for the sake of the people, pretending to be soldiers. They see nothing and hear nothing. They do not look for a fight with anyone. Los Federales are paid very little money. They have no heart for being soldiers because they are so poor."

"It don't appear anybody has any money down here," Slocum observed, casting a look around at signs of poverty everywhere his glance fell.

"This is the reason so many people listen to General Valdez. He promises them he will give them back land that once belonged to their ancestors if they join the revolution. Pedro says they are only empty promises. Señor Bustamante has always told me the same things, that General Valdez is nothing but a bandido who is telling the people lies.''

Slocum thought about Ramón's forthcoming meeting with Pedro, and perhaps with Victoriano Valdez. ''Tell Pedro to inform Valdez that I only want to discuss a price for the American girl he took at Laredo. Tell him the girl's father is willing to pay for her safe return. Be sure you tell him I'm not a lawman. I've only come here as a representative of the family to negotiate a price for seeing she gets back to Texas unharmed. Tell Valdez he can send someone to see me at the hotel, or I'll meet with him at any place of his choosing, so long as I've got some assurances he is coming to talk terms for the girl's release.''

Ramón nodded, wiping his plate clean with a tortilla. ''I will return late this afternoon if all goes well. I must talk to Pedro first and then Pedro will speak with the general. If the general wishes to arrange a meeting, he will send someone back with me who will talk with you personally, to see if you are telling the truth. Pedro says General Valdez is a very suspicious man. He will make sure los Federales have not followed me to his hiding place before he listens to what I have to say.''

''Be real careful you're not followed,'' Slocum warned. He signaled for their waiter and handed over silver when Ramón told him the price of their meal in American money.

They left the little café for a stroll down to the livery. As they were walking, Slocum thought about the risks facing the boy. He would have it on his conscience if Valdez did anything to Ramón. He'd grown to like the kid more and more as they got to know each other.

At a musty stable a few blocks from the hotel, Ramón

saddled his gray pony. Slocum kept an eye on the street until the boy was ready to leave. There had been no sign of Federale patrols in Saltillo since he saw them in front of the fort. Perhaps the boy was right, that these soldiers were merely putting on a show for the citizens of Saltillo, making them feel safe.

Ramón mounted and leaned out of his saddle. "I will be back before it is dark, señor. If someone is with me, it will be one of the general's men, so do not be alarmed. I will come straight to the hotel."

Slocum thumbed back his hat so he could see the boy's face. "Don't turn your back on anybody up there, son. And be sure you tell them I'm not a lawman. I'm only here to pay money for the girl's safe return. Make damn sure you tell 'em that part, so nobody will think I'm a bounty hunter or a peace officer."

Ramón trotted his pony out of the livery, turning west. It had been Slocum's idea all along to see which general direction the boy rode.

He walked back toward the plaza, idly listening to Spanish being spoken all around him. Glancing over his shoulder now and then, he made his way across the plaza to a narrow side street running up a steep hill toward the fortress. From there he would have a view of the mountains in every direction. The little gray mustang would be easy to see against a green mountainside.

A few minutes later, standing on a street corner across from the fort, Slocum gave what might pass for a grin. A dappled pony galloped due south away from Saltillo with a rider leaning over its neck. Ramón had changed directions, trying to throw him off by heading west when he left the stable. "Maybe that kid's smart enough to stay alive after all," he muttered under his breath.

Facing a long day with nothing much to do, Slocum decided to locate the telegraph office Tom told him about, take a hot bath, then saddle one of his horses for a tour of the countryside. He liked what he saw of the green mountain scenery around Saltillo, a pleasant change from the bleak desert he'd crossed to get here.

Sauntering casually down to the plaza so as not to appear to be anything more than a sightseeing visitor, he turned north when he saw a row of telegraph poles coming down the side of a distant mountain. The poles ran to a small adobe building at the north edge of town. Passing time, he walked up a hill to the front of the telegraph office, peering through a window as he went past. An elderly man in shirtsleeves sat at a desk where a telegraph key and a hand-cranked generator rested in front of him.

"That's all I needed to know," Slocum said quietly, as he walked around a corner of the building. "Only thing is, I sure hope that old man speaks some English."

He returned to the hotel and spent almost an hour in a cast iron tub in a bathhouse occupying a room off the back. A dark woman with Indian features carried pails of steaming water to him and later, clean towels. When he was shaved and dressed in his clean shirt, he strolled down to the livery, leaving his shotgun and rifle hidden under the mattress in his room. If he happened upon a Federale patrol, he didn't want to appear too heavily armed to be a casual visitor.

The sorrel seemed to be the fresher of his mounts and he put his saddle on it, ignoring curious looks an old liveryman gave him as he paid his board bill for another night. It was doubtful Saltillo received many American travelers since it was off the main roads from Monterrey to Mexico City or Torreon. Mounting up outside the stable, Slocum chose to ride in a southerly direction to see the lay of the land where Ramón had ridden. If negotiations with Valdez went awry, it could be helpful to know where a few trails led, just in case he needed to make a hurried exit with bullets flying over his head.

He rode through the city at a walk, admiring old buildings as any stranger might. Several people gave him lingering stares when he rode past. At the outskirts of town, he took a road due south, taking note of every offshoot trail heading into the hills leading up to steeper mountains. On many of the higher slopes he saw herds of goats and sheep, a few cattle, most of them the milking variety. He passed a few horsemen and an occasional donkey cart heading into town, but for the most part the road was empty.

Where the road climbed the side of a mountain, he passed one of the more elegant older homes around Saltillo, made of cut rock and mortar with archways for windows. A stone cutter had carved a number of floral designs around doorways and window openings. It was an impressive house, larger than any he'd seen. A woman was outside tending to flower gardens. She watched Slocum ride by with a hint of suspicion, as if she knew he didn't belong here.

As he was cresting the top of a ridge running up the side of a mountain where the road dropped sharply into a narrow ravine, he almost ran headlong into a column of soldiers. A Federale patrol was entering this same ravine from the south and when he saw them, he wheeled his sorrel off the skyline as quickly as he could. A narrow goat trail ran east into a line of piñon pines and he urged his horse to a gallop, hoping to make those trees before the Federales reached the top of the ridge. Asking the horse for all its speed, he drummed his heels into the gelding's ribs until pine limbs brushed his face and arms. Winding along a switchback, the trail plunged into a rocky gorge where it continued eastward. Slocum wasn't taking any chances with a run-in with the Mexican army. He kept his sorrel in a steady lope down this twisting canyon, hoping to outdistance the soldiers if one of them had happened to spot him when he wheeled off that ridge. If the Federales detained him to question him about his presence in Saltillo, it could spell doom for his chances of negotiating Melissa Anderson's release. It was a risk Slocum simply couldn't afford to take if he could prevent it.

An hour of travel down the rocky canyon brought him to one of the most beautiful mountain streams he'd ever seen, including some truly breathtaking sights in parts of Colorado or Wyoming. A tiny waterfall shed sparkling water into a crystal pool at the back of an offshoot arroyo running into the canyon he rode. He had been riding at a walk, after making sure he wasn't being followed by soldiers. He first glimpsed the waterfall through a thick stand of piñons and slender oaks. Halting his sorrel, he got down to lead it among the trees for a better look at this pretty spot when he suddenly noticed a pair of burros tied to a limb of an oak tree beside the pool beneath the falls. Then he saw two swimmers, heads bobbing on the surface, and in the next instant he heard laughter . . . girlish laughter.

For a moment, he stood hidden in the trees, watching a pair of young women splashing each other with handfuls of water and laughing. He knew by their bronze faces they were Mexican girls and once in a while he heard a word or two in Spanish, although the distance was too great for him to hear clearly. After a short deliberation, Slocum decided to approach the pool to make his presence known.

He led his sorrel to a piñon and tied it, making as little noise as he could. Unbuckling his gun belt, he looped it over his saddle horn and tucked his belly-gun inside one of his saddlebags. Showing up at the pool carrying weapons might frighten the two young women, and he didn't want to spoil their fun. Walking on the balls of his feet, he went quietly through the trees to the burros, then to the edge of the forest. There, on a flat rock beside the shimmering pool, he saw two dresses neatly folded and two pairs of sandals. In the sunlit water, both girls continued to play and swim without noticing him. After making sure no one else was nearby, he crept to the edge of the trees.

When he walked out into the sunlight, one of the girls saw him and screamed, *"Mira!"* and pointed at him.

The other girl stopped splashing and whirled around to face Slocum with sheer terror in her eyes.

"Uno gringo!" she cried. *"Peligroso! Fugarse!"*

Slocum raised his palms. "I won't hurt you," he said, as he took another few steps closer to the water. "I don't speak much *Español,* but I promise I don't mean you any harm."

Both women looked at their clothes, then at their burros. They would have to come toward Slocum to get their animals and put on their dresses.

He smiled and took off his hat to show his friendly intentions. "Don't be afraid of me. I only wanted to swim in this pretty pool for a while, to cool off." He hoped they understood him, for he was unable to say what he wanted to say in Spanish.

Several seconds passed. The girls glanced at each other and said nothing.

To show what he wanted, he placed his hat on a rock, opened buttons on his bib front shirt, and pulled it over his head. He put it beside his hat and began pulling off one of his stovepipe boots, having trouble balancing on one foot. Just as his boot was about to come free, he lost his balance and sat down hard on his rump, wincing when his buttocks landed on rocks.

One girl giggled. The other smiled. Slocum tossed his boot aside and pulled off the other, noticing for the first time how pretty the girls were, looking so much alike they could have been sisters, even twins.

13

Decency demanded that he keep on his denims when he got up to wade into the pool. At first the girls swam away from him as he entered shallower water, but he continued smiling and did not move directly toward them, angling for a spot below the falls to convince them he meant no harm. Both women were careful to keep themselves covered so that only their faces showed above the top of the waterfall pool.

"I won't hurt you," he promised again, trying to remember a way to say what he wanted in Spanish. "*No molestar*," he added, knowing his Anglo accent might make even his limited Spanish very difficult to understand.

He came to waist-deep water and knelt, enjoying the cool wet feeling against his skin. "*Frío*," he said, the word for cold.

One girl giggled again. She looked at the other. "You no speak *Español* good, gringo. Me no speak *Inglés* good. Is funny, no?"

"Yes, it's funny. I only came for a swim. I won't harm you, and that's a promise." He noted that both girls still remained submerged so only their heads and shoulders could be seen. "My name is John Slocum. I came down from Texas on a cattle buying trip. I thought I'd ride some back country and see the sights. This sure is a pretty place. Do you come here often?"

The girl who had spoken to him shook her head. "In summer. When is . . . hot . . . is right word?"

"Hot's the right word. What are your names?" he asked, not making any move to get closer to them for now, merely lounging in calmer waters near the falls.

The same girl answered him. "I am Anna. My sister is named Annabella. She no speak *Inglés*. I speak only a little."

"You are both very pretty," he told them.

Annabella, the girl who spoke no English, asked her sister, "*Que dicho?*" asking what Slocum said.

Anna answered in rapid Spanish. Annabella looked at Slocum and smiled. "*Gracias, señor, y usted es muy guapo,*" saying he was very handsome.

"*Gracias, señorita,*" he said. Grinning broadly, he suddenly felt playful. Cupping water in his hand, he sprayed each of them and laughed.

Both girls giggled and threw water at him. A water fight soon developed between them, splashing back and forth amid more laughter. Silver spray caught reflected sunlight as they sent handfuls of water at each other until Slocum's head was soaking wet. He noticed that both girls were moving closer, although they still remained below the surface up to their chins. He had a hunch they were both naked, yet neither one was willing to show herself during the splashing.

"Enough!" he cried, holding up his hands in mock surrender. "You will drown me." He stood up and wiped water from his face and eyes, finding the pool less than waist deep where he stood now.

Anna said something in Spanish to Annabella, words

Slocum didn't understand. Then, very slowly, Anna stood up, revealing she had nothing on. Her breasts were quite large and firm, glistening with tiny droplets of water. She had a small waist, making her breasts seem even bigger. She smiled, showing off perfect white teeth. Her long brown hair clung wetly to her back and shoulders. She gave Annabella a sideways glance. Reluctant at first, Annabella stood up beside her sister, covering rosy red nipples with tiny hands. Her breasts were larger than Anna's, melon-sized, quivering when she moved, like mounds of golden egg custard cast in a baker's mold.

"Is no fair," Anna said, wearing a pouty expression with a suggestion of laughter in her eyes. "You have *pantalones*. How you say in *Inglés*?"

"Pants," he answered back, reaching for the top button on his denims. "I'll take them off . . ."

Annabella seemed a bit frightened while he was slipping his pants down, until Anna said something to her in Spanish. When he got them off and tossed them to the edge of the pool, the tip of his swelling erection rose above the surface, just enough so both girls saw the head of his blood-engorged member.

Anna drew in a quick breath. "It is . . . *muy grande*," she said in a whisper. "*Muy, muy grande.*"

Annabella's eyes grew rounder while she stared down at his swollen prick. "*Verdad, es muy grande,*" she agreed.

Slocum admired both girls' magnificent breasts, small waists, and pretty faces. He cast an eye toward a shaded spot where deep grass grew below limbs of an oak tree. "We can dry off over there where it's cooler, out of the hot sun," he suggested.

Anna's dark eyes hooded with suspicion. "You no be *uno malo hombre*? No . . . bad man?"

"I'm not a *malo hombre*. I'm a cow buyer. I only suggested we lie down on that grass yonder to dry off before we put on our clothes."

Annabella whispered something to her sister. Anna gave him a look of appraisal, then her expression softened. She nodded to Annabella and turned, starting out of the pool, wading toward the grassy bank Slocum had indicated. Annabella followed until they reached the shallows, allowing him a view of their rounded hips and the tops of smooth thighs. Both girls had waist-length hair hanging damp against their backs. Slender waists gave both girls figures reminding Slocum of an hourglass.

He waded slowly behind them, thoroughly enjoying a rear view of Anna and Annabella, wondering how the fates could be so kind to him. He'd been riding hell-for-leather to avoid being found by a Federale patrol when suddenly he'd come upon a mountain stream where two beautiful Mexican maidens were bathing. It was a stroke of marvelous luck. And the girls were sisters, looking so much alike it was hard to tell them apart. Now he began to ponder how he might separate one from the other long enough to sample either one of the sisters' charms.

Anna came out on the bank ahead of Annabella, and when she turned to face Slocum, he caught his breath. Her body was even more spectacular when seen in its entirety. She had full hips and slightly rounded thighs, shapely calves, and slim ankles. A tuft of dark brown hair covered her mound. Her stomach was flat with only a suggestion of roundness in front. But it was when he gazed at her bosom that he found he could not take his eyes away. She had perfectly shaped breasts rising proudly from her rib cage that seemed to defy gravity. Her nipples were twisted into tiny buds.

When Annabella walked out of the pool, he was forced to take his eyes from Anna, for merely a glimpse of Annabella's pendulous breasts was enough to distract him.

Her bosom was heavy, almost oversized for the rest of her body. She was slimmer through the hips than her sister, although in good proportion, and when she turned to look at him, he became so fascinated by her profile in the sunlight that he stumbled over a submerged rock and almost lost his footing.

Annabella saw this and laughed. She spoke to Anna in words he didn't comprehend as he was staggering rather awkwardly out of the water. Then he realized his prick was standing erect and in a moment of uncharacteristic embarrassment he tried to cover it with both hands, until the girls' laughter became so infectious he laughed along with them and let his hands fall to his sides.

His erection pulsed, and all laughter stopped. For a time, Anna and Annabella simply stared at his throbbing cock. It was Annabella who came forward first, taking small, hesitant steps to reach him. She gazed down at his prick, beads of water running down her breasts, her stomach, her thighs. A slow smile brought tiny crow's feet to the skin around her eyes. She reached for his cock with a small brown hand and touched it lightly, only the tips of her fingers caressing his foreskin ever so gently.

"That feels good," he said, a tingle racing up the shaft of his prick to his balls.

It was as if Annabella understood his English. She knelt on the grass before him and opened her mouth, moving her fingers to the base of his member. Her pink tongue flicked out, licking the head of his cock once.

"Ah," he whispered, half closing his eyes in ecstasy while gazing down at her generous bosom.

A movement to his right caught his attention in spite of a wish to concentrate on what Annabella was doing. Anna came over to him, cupping a hand underneath her left breast, offering her nipple to him, placing it near his lips.

He bent down and took her nipple in his mouth, began sucking it, rolling the hardened nipple between his teeth. She moaned as his tongue encircled it. He noticed that she quivered with sheer pleasure and excitement while his tongue was at work.

But a stronger sensation awakened feeling in his throbbing prick when he felt Annabella's lips close around it. She began sucking noisily, curling her tongue around the end of his cock, bobbing her head back and forth, taking his member deeper and deeper into her throat. Slocum's knees started to feel weak. He wondered how long he could stand. Warmth in his testicles became heat and for a moment he was afraid his balls would explode in Annabella's hot, wet mouth.

When those feelings of ecstasy became too intense, he sank to his knees in the grass very slowly, clinging to Anna's breast with both hands while holding her nipple between his lips. And he felt, rather than saw, Annabella suck his cock into her mouth as he lay over on his side, then flat on his back.

"That feels so good," he moaned, briefly closing his eyes.

Anna pressed her breast against his face, almost smothering him when her soft bosom enveloped his nostrils. "Lick it harder, *mi gringo guapo*," she hissed, clenching her teeth as though she were in pain.

He bit down on her nipple, working the end with the tip of his tongue, wagging it back and forth. As he was doing this, he felt Annabella take his cock farther down her throat and she was wriggling her tongue around the head of his prick so furiously he was certain that his testicles would erupt. Annabella made slurping sounds while she sucked his cock, and when he glanced down, he saw saliva running from both corners of her mouth.

When he least expected it, Annabella swung her leg

over his chest, poising her moist cunt over the tip of his member. She parted the lips of her pussy with two fingers and pressed her mound over his prick.

He could feel how wet and warm her cunt was in the fraction of a second before she thrust herself downward, taking the length of his shaft inside her. He heard her cry out yet he could not see her because of Anna's breast pressed against his face. Anna ran her fingers through his hair, making fists, drawing his mouth to her twisted nipple by pulling his hair, moaning with desire.

Annabella started to grind her pelvis against the base of his prick, slowly, accompanied by groans of delight. She began to increase the speed and intensity of her thrusts, rubbing her hairy mound up and down his cock. Slocum tried to hold back as Annabella worked her cunt up and down, her hips slapping against his balls when she lowered herself completely onto the full thickness of his member.

"Damn . . . that feels . . . so good," he mumbled, his mouth filled with Anna's nipple.

Annabella's rhythm increased tremendously, hammering her wet pussy against his groin. He heard her stifle a cry, as though it was brought on by hurt, then she opened her mouth and gasped in ecstasy when she reached her climax.

His balls were afire, set to explode, when he felt Annabella slump to one side of him, collapsing on the grass. Slocum opened his eyelids just in time to see Anna climb aboard his stiff prick an instant after her sister's release.

Anna's gaze was fixed on his face and there was a faraway look in her eyes. She lowered her cunt over his member and sent it deep, uttering small sounds from her throat as each inch of his cock filled her womb. When she reached the hilt, she began to rock back and forth, each stroke more powerful, more demanding.

Slocum watched her breasts sway while she drove her-self to the base of his prick. He knew he could not hold his own orgasm much longer, yet he wanted to please Anna the way he'd pleased her sister. Arching his spine, he rammed his cock into her with all his might, meeting each of her thrusts with his own.

"Oh, oh," Anna cried, her nostrils flaring with each deep breath she took.

He increased the speed of his thrusts when he felt his balls rising—there was nothing he could do to prevent a climax now as the heat within his scrotum became un-bearably delightful. With all the strength he had, he ham-mered his cock into her and only a few moments later, his testicles emptied, shooting a fountain of jism into An-na's cunt. Straining, every muscle in his body gone tight, he experienced a powerful, wonderful release.

Slocum was panting, out of breath, held to the grass by the weight of Anna's body when his seed was finally spent. He stared up at her, at her remarkably beautiful face. Annabella was lying beside him, her forehead nes-tled into the nape of his neck. Her eyes were closed.

Anna bent down to kiss him lightly on the lips. "You good lover, gringo," she said.

He tried to think of something to say, but right then words got tangled up on the tip of his tongue and he simply lay there staring at two beautiful sisters, thinking that never before in his life had his luck been quite this good.

14

Slocum bid the two lovely sisters farewell after spending a couple of hours relaxing with them by the waterfall. They talked as best they could with their limited knowledge of the other's language while Anna served as interpreter between Slocum and Annabella. In the course of their conversation, he discreetly made inquiry as to the revolution in northern Mexico, saying he'd read about it in Texas newspapers. A look passed between Anna and Annabella, then Anna gave him a bit of important information he might be able to use later on. The tiny village of Nava below Saltillo was where young men went who wished to join the revolution. Nava was merely a spot on the map in the Sierra Madres, a very old village established more than a century ago by the early Spaniards trying to teach Christianity to the Yaqui Indians. It was hidden in a high mountain valley so remote that only someone who knew the region could find it.

"I wouldn't want to go there accidentally while I'm looking for cattle to buy," he'd said. "I wouldn't want to get shot by revolutionaries. I'll be heading south. How can I avoid getting too close to Nava?"

Anna explained. "When you ride between two tall

mountains, no ride trail climb to west. Trail go very high. Many rocks in trail. Go like snake up mountain. You no ride this trail.''

He nodded that he understood. ''I don't want to wind up in the middle of a revolution. Thanks for the warning.''

He'd ridden off in the direction of Saltillo after spending one of the most wonderful afternoons of his life. Bedding the two lovely sisters had been an experience he knew he would never forget. Guiding his sorrel back up the canyon, he remembered how perfect it had been making love to two women in such a beautiful setting, surrounded by trees at the waterfall, a golden sun beaming into the ravine. While the risks of coming to this part of Mexico on what was sure to be a dangerous mission were great, so were the rewards he had found thus far.

When he reached the main road back to Saltillo, he was doubly careful to look for army patrols before he struck out at a trot toward town. Wagon traffic and occasional horsemen passed both ways as he came closer to the city. Sighting the fortress, he didn't see any soldiers moving in or out of the gate. It was the middle of the afternoon, time for the traditional siesta in Mexico. If his luck held, he would be able to get back to the hotel without being noticed by Federales.

At the livery he put his horse away and handed the stable keeper a few small coins. The man paid some notice to his gun and holster, although not in apparent alarm. Slocum strode toward the plaza under a hot sun, thinking how good a few shots of whiskey would taste. Pedestrians he passed along the road paid little attention to him, even though his dress and general appearance was very different from theirs. As far as he knew, he was the only American in Saltillo at the moment, and this fact had begun to worry him a little. Word that a foreigner was in town might reach the *comandante* at the fort. Would the Federales be interested enough to question him about his reasons for being there?

He entered his hotel by a side door, a precaution in case Federales already knew of his presence and were watching for him to return to his room. He found the hotel lobby empty and made for the stairs, taking them two at a time. Walking softly down a poorly lit hallway, he fumbled for his key and unlocked the door. Just as he stepped inside his room, he saw a blur of rapid movement to his right.

Something crashed into his skull, sending him spinning to the floor. He clawed for his gun, his vision clouded by winking lights from the blow to his head. Whirling over on his side, he aimed his Peacemaker toward a shadowy shape towering over him and quickly tightened his finger on the trigger.

A boot struck his gun hand, knocking the Colt from his grasp before he could get off a shot. His gun went clattering into a corner of the room, but not before Slocum crawfished backward as fast as he could, reaching into his shirt for the .32 belly-gun. In a flash he had his smaller gun cocked, ready to fire, and the sound of a cocking pistol stopped the figure looming above him from coming any closer.

"I'll kill you!" Slocum swore, his head still reeling from being struck. "One step closer and I'll make a hole through your belly." He inched farther backward, trying to clear his brain and his vision quickly enough to get off a perfectly aimed shot. A swarthy Mexican crouched a few feet away, most of his face obscured by the wide brim of a drooping felt sombrero. A pair of crisscrossed bandoliers heavy with brass cartridges adorned his chest. He held a long-barreled pistol in his right fist with its muzzle aimed down at Slocum.

"I shoot you first," the Mexican snarled.

Slocum knew he couldn't back down. "Maybe. But I'll get off a shot and a belly wound is a hell of a slow way to die. I don't know who you are and don't give a damn. I swear, I'll kill you unless you lower that pistol and start explaining what you're doing in my room. And why you tried to bust open my skull like that."

For a fleeting moment, the heavy Mexican remained frozen in a crouch, gun covering Slocum. Then he slowly lowered the muzzle of his weapon. "I am from General Victoriano Valdez. You sent a boy to us with a message about money you will pay for this gringo woman with yellow hair. General Valdez will hear what you have to offer, but only if you come unarmed. Unless you give me your weapons, you will not be allowed to talk to the general."

Still keeping a close eye on the Mexican's gun, Slocum felt a knot on the back of his head, touching it gingerly with the tip of a finger on his free hand. "I'm not so sure I want to go someplace I've never been without my guns. This could be a trick, so you can rob me. I'll warn you now that I'm not carrying money to be offered for the girl's release. I'm supposed to wire a friend in Laredo as soon as the deal can be arranged. Someone will have to bring the girl closer to the border, so there won't be any chance of a double cross on either side. You show me the girl, and I'll hand over the money, if we can agree upon a price."

"The general will not come to the border."

"He came once, when he stole Howard Anderson's horses and took his daughter. Anderson doesn't want his horses back. All he wants is that girl safe on the north side of the Rio Grande."

Again, the big Mexican stated flatly, "General Valdez will not come to the border. Some other arrangement must be made if you wish to see the woman alive."

Very slowly, Slocum sat up from resting on an elbow. "We can talk about that, I reckon. But I'm not going anyplace where I'm unarmed until I'm sure this isn't a trick. I told you before I'm not carrying any money, just a letter from a bank in Laredo stating that the money is there, ready to be paid if I give the word a deal has been made." He remembered Ramón, wondering why the boy hadn't returned. "Where is the boy I sent to see General Valdez? I need to know he's okay."

"He is with the general. General Valdez will not come here to Saltillo for obvious reasons. The Federale garrison is here, and we are fighting for our freedom against the Federales. You must come with me, but only if you surrender all of your weapons. I took the rifle and shotgun you had hidden under your bed. You must give me the little *pistola*, and the gun I kicked from your hand."

It appeared that the only way to talk business with Valdez was on his own terms, yet the risks were tremendous. If Valdez wanted, he could have Slocum executed if negotiations went sour. It was grim news to learn that his Winchester and shotgun had already been seized. Armed with nothing but a pair of handguns, he was all but defenseless should things turn into an armed confrontation.

The Mexican spoke in a hoarse whisper. "If I meant to kill you, señor, you would be dead now. When you came into the room I could have killed you easily."

What the man said was true. If Valdez planned an ambush for him, it would have been all too easy for the Mexican to shoot him the moment he carelessly opened his door. "I suppose that part of what you say makes sense. I walked in here without thinking. I got this bump on my head instead of a bullet."

A look of satisfaction crossed the Mexican's face for only an instant. "So you see, I am not here to kill you, señor. I am only to take you to see General Valdez. But there can be no guns if you wish to talk about the woman. If you are as you say, here to make the general an offer, then there is no need for a gun.''

A thousand thoughts raced through Slocum's mind at once. It went against his grain to face any situation without a means of defending himself, yet it appeared this was the only way he could meet with the bandits who held Melissa Anderson prisoner. It was a risk he ordinarily wasn't willing to take. He decided he would be forced to live by his wits until he was in a position to set conditions. ''I suppose it doesn't leave me with much of a choice in the matter,'' he said, relaxing his grip on the .32. ''If this is the only way, then it's pretty cut and dried. Either I give you my guns, or there'll be no discussion about paying ransom for the girl.''

''This is the only way, señor. Give me the little *pistola* so we can be on our way to see the general.''

Slocum took a deep breath and let it out slowly, in resignation. He'd come this far trying to arrange the girl's release. A pair of pistols wouldn't save his life, anyway, in a shoot-out with an army of bandits. If he traded bullets with Valdez's emissary now, the best he could hope for was a lucky shot through a vital organ, then a fast escape out of Saltillo ahead of the Federales after shots were heard at the hotel. ''It seems you're holding all the aces. Here's my gun,'' Slocum said, lowering the hammer on his .32 with his thumb, offering it flat on his palm.

The Mexican took his pistol, walking over to the wall where Slocum's Colt .44 lay. When both guns were stuffed into the bandit's belt, he nodded to Slocum. ''Now we can go,'' he said.

Slocum picked up his hat before he climbed unsteadily to his feet, his head still reeling from the blow. Placing his Stetson gently atop his skull to avoid the swelling, he motioned to his saddlebags piled in a corner of the room.

"I could use a drink of whiskey after getting my head smashed. There's a bottle in my gear over yonder. No gun, just whiskey."

The Mexican inclined his head. He still held his pistol at his side, proving he didn't entirely trust Slocum. "Bring the whiskey," he said, "and this letter telling about the money in Laredo."

Slocum clumped over to his saddlebags and fished out the pint, then an envelope from the Cattleman's Bank. Folding the letter into a shirt pocket, he pulled the cork and took a thirsty swig of sour mash. A dull pain radiated from the knot on his head to the base of his neck. Another pull from the bottle helped take his mind off his throbbing skull for the moment. "That's better. My head hurts like hell. Wish you hadn't hit me quite so damn hard . . ."

From the corner of his eye, Slocum saw the Mexican holster his pistol.

"My orders were to take your guns or your life, señor. A bump on the head is far better than a bullet hole. I am called Ortega. When we go down the stairs, remember that I will be behind you. Do not be so foolish as to try to run away. I will kill you if you try to run. Those are my orders."

Slocum put the pint in his pants pocket. "You speak good English, Ortega. I understand what'll happen if I try anything. I'm only interested in arranging for the girl's release. Nothing else matters to me."

Ortega motioned to the door. "Someone will meet us at the stable. Your horse has been saddled. It is time to go."

Slocum walked out into the hallway first, feeling naked without a gun. "I'll lock the door," he said, putting his key to the lock as soon as Ortega came out.

"Take the back stairs," Ortega commanded, keeping his voice low. "Walk down the alley and say nothing to anyone we meet on the way to the stable. I will be right behind you. A bullet so close will break your spine, se-ñor.''

Slocum went to the end of the hallway as quietly as he knew how, to a door opening above a set of steps leading down to an alleyway heaped with garbage. Stray dogs nosed through piles of refuse as the two men descended the stairway. The odor of decay filled their nostrils when they reached the bottom step.

''That way,'' Ortega said, pointing west.

Stepping wide of garbage heaps, Slocum started down the alley, holding his breath from the stench. He could hear Ortega's heavy boots close behind him. They came to a side street where Slocum turned south without re-ceiving instructions, for he knew the way to the stable now.

A few bystanders gave them curious stares as they walked to the livery. Some seemed to recognize Ortega. Whispered words were spoken by a few when they saw Ortega, yet no one gave him a sign of recognition, a wave, or a friendly smile. Slocum could only guess they knew him and feared him as an associate of the revolutionary general's.

At the stable they were met by a tall Mexican who carried two pistols at his waist. Slocum didn't like the man's appearance at all—he had close-set, nervous black eyes and a perpetual scowl on his face. He figured to be the more dangerous of the two, judging by the look of him, the way he carried himself, and his habit of contin-ually watching his surroundings. He handed Slocum the reins to his sorrel, then he spoke to Ortega.

''Vamos. Andale!''

''Sí, Juanito,'' Ortega said, mounting a dun gelding with a Bar A, Howard Anderson's brand, on its left rump.

Juanito climbed aboard a chestnut with a similar brand.

Valdez's men had obviously put Anderson's blooded horses to good use.

Slocum mounted and rode out of the livery flanked by the two Mexicans, believing he was headed toward one of the most dangerous encounters of his career since the war. Worst of all, he was unarmed, except for the Bowie knife hidden in his boot. A knife wouldn't be much help, he knew, surrounded by scores of Mexican bandits carrying guns.

15

They rode side streets, pausing at every street corner, and Slocum knew Ortega and Juanito were watching for Federales. Slocum took every opportunity to size up his escorts when their attention was elsewhere. A sideways glance at Juanito further convinced him he was the most dangerous. Juanito carried a modified Walker Colt in a cutaway holster tied low on his leg, a rig designed for speed at the draw. Ortega was a bullish man who would be awkward with a fast pull. However, Slocum needed no reminder of how well Ortega wielded a pistol for a club. The knot on Slocum's head throbbed with each movement of his sorrel as they trotted down back roads out of Saltillo. Given a choice of adversaries, though, he would much prefer to battle Ortega with almost any weapon, including fists, for the big Mexican's movements were slow, just slow enough to give Slocum an edge. And as an aside, he owed Ortega for that blow to his skull, adding a bit of anger and revenge to a choice between fighting one or the other. Under any other circumstances, he wouldn't let a thing like that pass without getting even.

Near the edge of town, as they were riding through one of the poorest sections where tiny adobe shacks were crowded together on narrow dirt lanes, Slocum discovered that his shotgun and Winchester were being carried in a canvas sling on the off side of Juanito's horse. Ortega had searched his room while he was with the lovely sisters, Anna and Annabella, confiscating his weapons and probably anything else of value in his saddlebags, including his boxes of ammunition. An afternoon's sweet ecstasy had cost him precious time away from the hotel and his weapons. Silently he cursed his stupidity for allowing himself to be sidetracked by two beautiful women. He'd come to Saltillo on business and permitted pleasure to get in the way. But in honest self-examination, he knew he'd been guilty of this same weakness for the better part of his life, and it was pointless to languish in feelings of remorse. Under any circumstances he would have done the same thing again, should he run across pretty maidens bathing naked in a stream. Beautiful women had been his downfall all too often, getting him in one scrape after another, yet he had few, if any, regrets. He had known some of the most beautiful women west of the Mississippi in intimate ways most men only dreamed about, and thus far he was still alive to tell about his adventures.

But the forthcoming meeting with Victoriano Valdez could be his comeuppance. He'd allowed himself to be disarmed by the men who were taking him there. Never before could he recall heading into what he knew would be a potentially deadly situation without any way to defend himself.

They rode out of town into a forest of piñon pines, where Ortega swung his dun horse west, angling for the road Slocum had ridden that took him south earlier in the day. Ortega rode out in front with Juanito bringing up the rear, sandwiching Slocum between them. As soon as they had ridden barely a quarter mile, they came to the rutted wagon road, and as Slocum predicted, they turned south.

Slocum thought they were headed for Nava, the village Anna told him about. He wondered how Ramón had fared in the bandit gang's stronghold. He hoped the boy was okay—funny, that he would have thoughts like this over a Mexican kid who had tried to rob him.

Ortega urged his horse to a lope and Slocum hurried his own gelding to stay close. One part of a possible plan Slocum might have employed to get the girl out of Mexico was worthless now, he knew. If somehow he could have gotten her away from Valdez by force or stealth and made a run for the border on better horses, he stood a chance of being able to outdistance men riding lesser animals. But with Valdez's men mounted on Howard Anderson's thoroughbred geldings, the race would be too close, too dangerous. The only hope of bringing the girl back to Texas was to pay whatever ransom money Valdez demanded for her. Even then, Valdez might double-cross them at the last minute. Nothing could be counted on until Melissa Anderson was across the Rio Grande.

The road climbed into mountains Slocum knew, past the old hacienda and its pretty flower gardens, then to the steep ravine where he had encountered the Federale patrol. Glancing to the east, his eyes roamed the slender trail he'd ridden this morning to the waterfall and the delightful sisters. In spite of the dangers he knew were ahead for him, he smiled when they galloped past the trail to the pool, remembering. It was an experience he was sure he would never forget.

They rode to the bottom of the ravine and out the far side at a gallop, until the road climbed more steeply, forcing their horses to labor for air. Ortega slowed to a trot and so did the other animals. Once, Slocum glanced over his shoulder. Juanito stared back at him with hard black eyes made of pitch. Slocum had no doubts that Juanito would enjoying killing him, should the need arise.

"I won't give him any excuse," Slocum whispered under his breath. "Not until I'm ready to make my move . . . if and when the time comes."

The road crested a rise, then plunged down a drop so steep their horses had to scramble for footing in spots worn down to loose rock by wagon wheels. Slocum's head ached, and when he remembered crashing to the floor of his hotel room, he ground his teeth together in anger. There were times when he prided himself on how well he controlled his temper, yet there were also times like these when he battled urges to forget everything else and settle things with Ortega.

They had ridden only an hour when they came to a pair of tree-studded mountains where a ribbonlike trail ran up the side of a slope heading west. This was the trail that Anna had told him led to Nava, he felt sure. The trail climbed so sharply that their horses could only navigate it at a walk, and even then they encountered difficult places where one horse or the other had to scramble to keep its footing. Slocum followed the trail with his eyes, seeing where it appeared to pass over the top of the peak in front of them. Surrounded by trees, the pathway was barely visible in some spots where it wound around slabs of bald rock or turned to avoid a climb too steep for any animal other than a mountain goat. By the looks of things, not many people ventured to Nava by this route. Idly, he wondered what they would find when they got there. Would it be an armed camp full of revolutionary patriots who believed in a cause, or simply a bandits' lair where ruthless men collected spoils they took in the name of revolution?

One thing became abundantly clear as they rode up the face of the mountain—there would be no possibility of a fast escape from Nava if he found a way to free the girl while he was here. No horse on earth could manage terrain like this in a hurry.

When he first glimpsed the tiny mountain village, Slocum thought it might be a mirage. Pale white walls surrounded a collection of buildings perched on the side of a mountain, and when the sun struck those walls, they appeared so white as to be unnatural, of a substance almost luminous. A forest of taller pines, not the piñon variety Ramón had showed him at lower elevations, surrounded the walled city. The deep green color of the pines made Nava's walls seem that much brighter. Until they came in sight of Nava, neither Ortega nor Juanito said a word, but when they rode over a forested ridge giving them a view of the city, Ortega turned back in the saddle and said, "When you speak to the general, call him General Valdez."

"I'll try to remember that," Slocum replied, hoping the sarcasm in his voice wasn't too evident.

Ortega gave him a mirthless grin. "If you do not remember, the general will have you shot, señor. Perhaps knowing this will help you remember."

Nothing more was said as they rode off the ridge and down a very steep drop into a narrow valley. Slocum never doubted Ortega's promise that Valdez would order him executed should he neglect protocol. Again, he felt naked without his guns, heading into a city full of armed desperados. A moment of carelessness when he entered his hotel room had cost him dearly, putting him at such a disadvantage that the only bargaining tool he had was an offer of ransom money. Dumb mistakes like this cost men their lives every day. Slocum hoped this wasn't his day to learn life's most important and final lesson in survival.

They rode through an opening in Nava's stone walls,

watched closely by half a dozen Mexicans with rifles. Forced to take a guess, Slocum would have figured fewer than four hundred people lived in Nava. No more than two dozen buildings occupied what limited space there was inside the walls: mostly dwellings, a few shops, and a market near the center of town. Another thing was immediately evident as soon as they rode in: the village was full of heavily armed men. Bearded Mexicans in sombreros eyed their arrival from doorways and windows all across the city. Guns of every description were tied to their waists or carried loosely balanced in the palms of their hands. Rifles and pistols, some old and some newer models, were carried by men walking narrow streets or lounging under shaded porches. Slocum hadn't seen so many guns since Gettysburg, or so many men who looked capable of using them at the slightest provocation.

Ortega led them to the largest building in Nava, the only one having two stories. Windows across the front of upstairs rooms had small balconies overlooking the street. Ortega rode to a hitch rail and swung down, motioning for Slocum to do likewise. To Slocum's left, Juanito got down off his chestnut without once taking his black eyes off Slocum, as though he expected trouble from him at any moment. It was wearing on Slocum's nerves, the way Juanito stared at him continually.

"Inside," Ortega said gruffly, aiming a thumb at a door into the front of the building, resting his other hand on the butt of his holstered pistol. "Someone will inform the general that we are here."

"Where's the boy, Ramón?" Slocum asked, tying his horse to the rail. "I'd like to see him before we meet with General Valdez."

Juanito spoke in a hoarse voice. "It is not for you to say when you meet the general, gringo. Go inside, or I put a gun to your head and kill you now."

Slocum gave Juanito an angry stare, then he shook his head and started for the door. Without a gun he would be forced to take whatever cards were dealt him, including their threats and insults.

Three armed guards watched their entrance into the building. They gave Slocum disinterested looks and he ignored them. He entered a room full of small tables and chairs with a bar across the back. Oil lamps hung from the rafters gave off meager light, casting shadows on a dirt floor. No one was seated at any of the tables. A bartender wiped a row of glasses on a shelf behind him with a piece of cloth.

"Sit here," Ortega ordered, indicating a table near a front window looking out on the street.

The place was quiet, making the sound of Slocum's boots the only noise when he walked over to the table and took a chair with his back to the wall. The room smelled faintly of stale beer and corn tortillas and other scents he couldn't readily identify. His chair was fashioned from pine limbs, covered with goatskin. The table was hand-hewn from rough planks, stained, initials carved in spots. Juanito came over to the wall and leaned against it so that he was close to Slocum's right shoulder. Ortega said a few words in Spanish to one of the guards, then he crossed the room and took a chair opposite Slocum.

The guard disappeared, walking through a door leading to a side room. Slocum heard boots climbing stairs.

"Tequila," Ortega said to the barkeep. He looked at Slocum with hooded eyes. "I have sent for the general. Until he comes, we drink tequila."

"I ain't all that particular," Slocum remarked, glancing out the window. "Never saw so many armed men, not since the war. I reckon I'm the only one in Nava without a gun."

Ortega's eyes slitted even more. "How is it you know

the name of this place?'' He bored through Slocum with a look awaiting an answer.

Slocum realized his mistake too late. ''I looked at a map and I took a guess while I was in Saltillo. The boy rode south and it didn't take much to figure where he'd be likely to go.''

Still suspicious, Ortega asked, ''Did you talk to anyone in Saltillo about where to find General Valdez?''

''I hardly speak any Spanish at all. Nobody I tried to talk to in Saltillo spoke much English. It was just a guess that this was Nava. I damn sure didn't talk to any Federales, if that is what you want to know. The Federales wouldn't take too kindly to an American nosing around down here, anyway. I was gonna tell them I was a cattle buyer if they questioned me.''

For the moment, Ortega seemed satisfied. He turned to watch the bartender bring them a bottle of tequila, a bowl of limes, and three shot glasses. When the bottle arrived, Ortega took out its cork and poured three drinks, then he tossed his shot of tequila back in a single gulp and poured another before Slocum had a chance to take a swallow.

Juanito came to the table and knocked back his drink. He declined to take any more when Ortega offered, returning to his place against the wall.

Boots sounded heavily on the stairs. Slocum watched the doorway leading into the adjoining room. Something told him he was about to meet the infamous Victoriano Valdez. He reminded himself to call the bandit chieftain a general.

16

A shadow fell across the floor just beyond the door into the next room. Slocum recalled what Tom Spence had said about Valdez, that he was considered one of the worst border cutthroats in the north of Mexico, almost legendary for his ability to elude capture by the Mexican army. Tom wouldn't have handed out that kind of warning without plenty of justification, being marshal of a town like Laredo, one of the toughest places anywhere. Slocum leaned back in his chair, waiting for Valdez to appear, certain the bandit leader would try to test him, to get at the truth. Valdez would expect a trick, a deception of some kind, as any careful man should. There would be hard questions and maybe some bluffing until the self-styled general was sure Slocum's ransom offer was genuine.

A man filled the doorway, heavy shoulders almost too broad to allow him to enter the room. A coarse black beard covered half of a round face and fleshy jowls. Powerful hands dangled at his sides near a brace of pistols. His hair fell to his shoulders in neglected curls, making him appear even more menacing, a wild look about him that would be unsettling to men who lacked experience dealing with tough types. He wore leather leggings, a sleeveless cotton shirt badly soiled by food stains and sweat, and stovepipe boots almost touching his knees.

"*Quien es*?" the Mexican asked, wanting to know who Slocum was, directing his question to Ortega. By his demeanor, he was accustomed to having authority, identifying him in Slocum's mind as Victoriano Valdez.

Ortega answered in Spanish. Although Slocum understood only a few of the words, he knew Ortega was explaining why Slocum was in Nava.

Valdez grunted, scowling, bushy eyebrows knitted together. A lengthy silence followed while he sized up Slocum without walking across the room. As Slocum was making his own appraisal of Valdez, he heard a gun being cocked close by. He knew it was Juanito who had cocked his gun. To show he had no fear of the gun, Slocum did not turn his head to look at Juanito's pistol.

"Stand up when General Valdez is here," Juanito demanded, as he aimed his revolver at Slocum's skull.

Gambling that Juanito would not shoot him without orders to do so from Valdez, Slocum sat still, meeting Valdez's cold stare. "I'd be glad to stand up and shake hands with him when he comes over to talk to me," Slocum replied evenly.

Hearing this, Valdez smiled crookedly, revealing a single gold tooth in the front of his mouth, yet there was no mistaking the smile for a sign of friendliness. "Are you brave, hombre? Or maybeso only *estupido*. Have you no fear of a gun?"

Slocum merely shrugged, showing courage he didn't actually feel right then. "I don't figure he'll shoot me without orders from you, General. And I don't figure you'll have me shot until you hear what I have to say about giving you money for the girl you took prisoner in Texas. The girl's father wants her back, and he's willing to pay. He don't care about the horses you stole. He can raise more horses, but that girl's his only daughter.''

Valdez's expression did not visibly change. "How much money do you bring to pay for her?''

"I didn't bring any. I'm here to negotiate for her release, and if we can agree on terms, I'll bring the money across the Rio Grande and deliver it to you personally.''

The general seemed to be thinking. "How much money will you give for this yellow-hair woman?''

"I've got a letter in my pocket from a bank in Laredo which authorizes me to offer five thousand dollars in gold for the safe return of Melissa Anderson to Texas. As soon as you bring her to a place we both agree on, I'll hand you the money, and I'll take her back to Laredo.''

"This place," Valdez began, "where is this place you want me to take her?''

"Someplace close enough to the border so I can make sure you won't change your mind. Once I've paid for her, I intend to keep her.''

Hearing this, Valdez left the doorway and sauntered over to Slocum's table, glaring down at him, hooking his thick thumbs in his gun belt. "Show me this letter," he said, making it sound as though he doubted its existence.

Slocum took the letter from his pocket, and handed it to Valdez while trying to keep his nose from wrinkling over the Mexican's unwashed smell. "I can verify everything it says in that letter by sending a wire from the telegraph office in Saltillo. The offer is genuine. Anderson wants his daughter back, and he'll pay five thousand dollars in American gold to get it done. The only conditions are that she is unharmed and that you bring her someplace close to the border. It's a straightforward proposition.''

Valdez opened the letter, looked at it, and handed it to Ortega. "Tell me what it say. Read it carefully," he warned.

Ortega squinted at the paper in poor light, eyes following each line written in careful longhand. "It say this man is John Slocum and he have authority to offer five thousand dollars in American gold for the return of Melissa Anderson to Laredo, in Texas, to be paid when she cross the Rio Grande. It say, telegraph sent to Cattleman's Bank in Laredo will be answered by a Mister Thomas Spence that this money will be paid to Victoriano Valdez in gold coins."

Valdez cast a suspicious look at Ortega, then at Slocum as he listened to the letter. "Letter say money paid when she cross Rio Grande. You say we meet close to border. Letter no say you give me gold before she cross river. Is no good, this letter."

"It's the wording. All it means is that the money will be given to you when you bring her to a place we agree upon—"

"*No bueno*!" Valdez shouted. "Letter must say we get money before yellow-hair woman cross river!"

"I can arrange to have that put in the message we get back from Laredo. If you'll send someone with me to the telegraph at Saltillo, I'll get you an answer stating the money will be paid as soon as we make the exchange, the girl for the gold."

It was quickly evident there was something about the proposed arrangement Valdez didn't like. "Words on piece of paper mean nothing, gringo. I must have proof there is gold. You bring this gold to me and I give you the woman. You come here. I count money. Then woman is yours."

"I can't do that, and you know why," Slocum protested. "It would be too dangerous for me to bring that kind of money down here, and then I'd have to ride more than a hundred miles to get back to the border. I don't know any of the back roads, and if the Federales found me with the money or the girl, there'd be too many questions. And I'd be taking a risk that you might change your mind and take the girl back once I gave you the money. I want some assurances that I can get the girl safely across the river to her father's ranch. It's just good business."

Valdez made like he took offense over Slocum's remark, a narrowing of his eyelids. "You insult me, gringo, saying you think I cheat you, I take this money and keep woman."

Slocum felt trapped, yet he knew he had to insist upon a meeting place near the border or there was a real chance Valdez would double-cross him. Doing some fast thinking, he said, "It wasn't my idea. Howard Anderson said he'd only pay the money if he had assurances that his daughter would be released close to the Rio Grande. Otherwise, he won't allow the bank to give me the gold. It probably has as much to do with the fact that he does not trust me. He may be worried that I'll ride off with his money and he'd never see his daughter again. I'm only acting as an agent, so to speak. He doesn't know me. We only met a few days ago. I was hired to negotiate the girl's release. I came down from Fort Worth to see if I could contact you and make the arrangements."

His answer seemed to satisfy Valdez for the moment. However, some doubts lingered. "Maybeso you take the gold and keep it for yourself, gringo. How much Señor Anderson pay you to come here to Nava?"

It was time to tell Valdez the truth. "He's paying me five thousand dollars, but only if he gets his daughter back. If she doesn't make it back to Texas, I get nothing."

A silence followed. In order to appear calm, Slocum poured himself a shot of tequila, corked the bottle, and tossed it back. Valdez watched his every move the way a cat watches a mouse. As he lowered his glass, Slocum said, "I have no stake in this. I came here for the money, to make a payday. If you're interested in Anderson's prop-

osition, I'll telegraph the bank in Laredo from Saltillo and
have the gold ready for an exchange. If you're not, I'll
ride back to Laredo and tell the girl's father that the deal
wasn't satisfactory, that you've decided to keep the girl.
It don't make any difference to me. I can't get paid unless
I get his daughter back to Texas alive. And there's one
more thing; I need to talk to the girl, so I can tell him
she's okay.''

Valdez had been listening closely to everything Slocum
said, and when he finished telling the general what the
conditions for an exchange would be, Valdez put the palm
of his right hand on the butt of his pistol.

"Five thousand for you. Five thousand dollars for me.
I have the woman. You have nothing, Señor Slocum. This
man in Laredo pays you too much for coming here.''

Not sure what to say, Slocum replied, ''It's the deal I
was offered. I didn't set the price.''

"Is not enough," Valdez said.

Ortega chuckled, looking at Valdez. ''This gringo make
too much money. If you say the word, Juanito will shoot
him. He is one dead gringo, *verdad*?''

"*Es verdad*," Valdez agreed, nodding once.

"I didn't set the price," Slocum told them again.

Valdez cast a wary look out the window to the street.
"I am an honorable man. You tell the father of this girl
that I sell her to him for ten thousand dollars in gold.''

"That's too high," Slocum said, wagging his head,
pouring a drink as though they were talking about the
weather. ''Anderson will pay five thousand. Not a dime
more.''

"He pay ten thousand," Valdez said. ''Five thousand
he pay to you, five he offer to me. If he want this yellow-
hair woman, he pay me ten thousand dollars in gold.''

"He won't do it," Slocum argued.

"Then his daughter will die," Valdez promised. ''You

send a telegraph message to him. Tell him he pay ten thousand in gold or I cut the woman's throat.''

"That doesn't leave anything for me," Slocum said, his mind racing. Would Valdez kill the girl?

"Is your problem," the general said. He gave Ortega a look. "Take Señor Slocum to *el oficina telegrafo*. Let him send this message to Laredo: Pay ten thousand dollars in gold for the girl or I will kill her, *prontito*!"

Ortega shook his head. "*Sí, jefe*. I will see that this is the message Señor Slocum sends to Laredo.''

"*Bueno*," Valdez agreed, stepping back, telling Slocum their conversation was ended.

Juanito nudged the base of Slocum's skull with the barrel of his pistol. "Get up, gringo. We ride back to Saltillo. You say words El General tell you say, or I kill you. *Comprende*?''

"I understand," Slocum muttered, pushing back his chair. "I don't think Howard Anderson will agree, but I'll send the message anyway.''

Valdez wore a satisfied look. "The father of this girl will agree to pay ten thousand dollars," he said, sounding very sure of it. "He know I will kill her if he say no.''

Slocum stood up, remembering Ramón Casillas. "I'd like to see the boy who brought you my message. Just to make sure he's okay. I didn't give him anything for coming here. He didn't do anything wrong.''

"The boy is dead," Valdez said. "I ordered one of my men to shoot him. He was a traitor to *la revolución*. He tell his cousin, Pedro, that he helped a gringo come to Saltillo to look for me. I had no choice, Señor Slocum. I must have men killed who tell others where we are.''

Slocum stiffened. "The kid didn't mean any harm. No reason to shoot him like that.''

Valdez grinned, showing off his gold tooth. "You no understand, gringo. Many people in Mexico try to find me. If anyone says where to look for me, *los* Federales will come. I gave the order to have this boy shot by a firing squad. All the people of Nava saw this execution. They will tell others what will happen to anyone who comes to Nava telling where we hide from the evil soldiers, *los* Federales.''

Hearing that Ramón had been executed by a firing squad, it was a reflex when Slocum made angry balls of his fists. ''The kid knew nothing,'' he said. ''You shot an innocent kid who only came to Nava bearing my message.''

Valdez had a gleam in his dark eyes when he replied, ''I do not shoot innocent people, Señor Slocum. The boy came here. He could have led *los* Federales to me. No one comes to Nava, or to any other place where we hide from *los soldados*. This boy you call Ramón knew this. He came knowing he risked his own life.''

Slocum lowered his head. Ramón had been killed for delivering a message at Slocum's request. It was mindless to shoot the boy for bringing a message to Nava. Now Ramón's death hung heavy on Slocum's conscience.

''We go now,'' Ortega said, motioning Slocum to the front door by inclining his head.

''I'll send that wire,'' Slocum said quietly, giving Valdez a look. ''Ten thousand is too much to ask for the girl, but I'll tell Howard Anderson it's your price.'' He trudged past Valdez to the door and walked out as a late afternoon sun slanted into the village. Mounting his horse, he made himself a promise. If he could, he would make Victoriano Valdez pay dearly for having the boy put before a firing squad.

17

It was dark by the time they reached Saltillo. Descending the mountains had worn their horses down and now they traveled with heads lowered, gaunt-flanked, needing water and rest. All the way back, when Slocum allowed his mind to wander, he thought about Ramón facing a firing squad for nothing more than bringing a message to Nava. Several times, remembering the boy, Slocum renewed his vow to make Valdez pay for murdering an innocent kid whose only crime had been carrying an offer of ransom money in Slocum's behalf to Valdez's hideout. He wondered how he would explain Ramón's fate to Señor Bustamante at the ranch, and too, if the boy had any family to grieve for him. It hadn't seemed wrong then to offer Ramón twenty dollars for riding to Valdez's hideaway merely to inform him of the ransom money, but the job had cost Ramón all he had and Slocum was to blame.

As before, Ortega took them into the city by back routes, avoiding main thoroughfares where they might be seen by Federale patrols. A few dogs barked when their horses trotted down dark streets in quiet neighborhoods, but otherwise their arrival in Saltillo went unnoticed.

By circling the heart of town, they approached the telegraph office from the north. The little building was dark, appearing to be closed for the night. Ortega led them to the rear by way of an alley where they climbed down from their saddles at a door leading into the back of the office.

Slocum's muscles were stiff after so many hours aboard his horse. Ortega and Juanito had hardly spoken during their ride out of the mountains. Ortega knocked on the door softly, after making sure no one saw them in the alley.

"*Quien es?*" a small voice asked from inside.

"Julio," was all Ortega said.

The door opened. The old man Slocum had seen in the telegraph office the day before peered out into the darkness.

Ortega spoke rapidly in Spanish. The old man stepped aside to allow them to enter. A lantern was lit, revealing they were in a tiny bedroom. The telegraph operator carried his lantern into a front room where his telegraph key and generator sat on a desk.

"What do you wish to say, and where do you want the message sent?" the old man asked in near perfect English, picking up a stub of a pencil, holding it above a piece of foolscap near the spot where he put his lamp.

"I want it sent to Laredo, Texas, in care of Tom Spence. I want you to say this: Howard Anderson must agree to pay ten thousand dollars in gold for the . . . merchandise he sent me down here to buy for him. Ten thousand in gold is the price. Ask to have an answer wired back here as soon as possible. Sign my name to it, John Slocum."

Writing slowly, it required several minutes for his message to be transcribed. Then the old man turned a hand crank on his generator a number of times, sat down, and tapped his telegraph key only a few strokes before he paused.

"They will answer in Monterrey if the line is working. This message must be sent to Monterrey first, then to Laredo. It will take time, a few hours."

Ortega spoke. "Tell me when the message has been sent. We wait at El Agave cantina for the answer to come. You bring it to us there, Miguel. Tell no one about this . . . no one!"

Miguel agreed silently, watching his telegraph key. A short time later, the key started to click, then it stopped. "The line is open to Monterrey. I will send this message *muy pronto*. When the answer comes, I bring it to El Agave."

Until then Juanito had been quiet. "Tell no one, old man," he said, hand resting on the butt of his pistol.

Ortega placed a fistful of pesos on the table. Juanito made a motion for Slocum to leave by the rear door. They walked out in silence, after Juanito carefully surveyed the alleyway for any sign of activity. Once aboard their horses, Ortega led them to the northeast, making another circle around the business district of Saltillo, keeping to deeper shadows wherever they could. It was plain by Ortega's actions that the only thing he feared was an encounter with Mexican soldiers. Otherwise, he made no special effort to avoid being seen by any local citizens when they rode through poor residential sections of the city.

Near the eastern edge of Saltillo they came to a squat adobe building with its windows alight. A few horses and burros were tied to rails across the front. Ortega took them to the back of the place where a three-sided shed was surrounded by crude pole corral.

"We leave our caballos here," he explained. "We wait for Miguel to bring us the answer from Laredo." He turned to Slocum and cocked his head. "For the sake of this woman, the answer is yes. If is no, the general will surely kill her, as he promised he would.''

Slocum had been worrying about what the wire would say and he hoped Tom would send a reply agreeing to Valdez's price, even if Howard Anderson balked over the amount. Tom should understand that what mattered most was getting Melissa close to the border unhurt. Hadn't Anderson said to offer Valdez as much as it would take to get his daughter back?

He was ushered into a quiet cantina where a few drinkers sat at small tables or stood at the bar. When they walked in, some patrons exchanged polite greetings with Ortega and Juanito, as if they were well known here. But when drinkers noticed an American in their midst, conversation stopped. For a few moments there was total silence, until Ortega motioned Slocum to an empty table close to a back door beside the bar. Only then did he notice that Juanito was waiting outside near the doorway, standing where he could keep an eye on the street.

"Tequila," Ortega told a plump young waitress. She hurried off to bring them a bottle of tequila and a dish of cut limes.

Slocum decided to try getting information from Ortega, any scrap he might use that could prove helpful if an exchange was arranged for the girl. "How many men ride with General Valdez?" he asked, making it sound casual.

Ortega gave him a cold stare. "Be silent, gringo. Do not ask me questions. Juanito has been begging me to let him kill you, telling the general you tried to escape. Drink some tequila and say nothing to make me angry."

"Have it your way," Slocum said, pouring a drink, then taking a slice of lime. He wished with all his heart that he had a gun right now. It wouldn't take much more provocation for him to turn the tables on Ortega and Juanito and Victoriano Valdez, despite what might happen to the Anderson girl as a result, if only he had a pistol and his rifle. He'd kept his temper in check about as long as he could. Biting into a lime, he tasted its bitter juice and tried to keep from remembering Ramón Casillas. Slocum's father had a favorite saying he often quoted to his sons when the family trait called Slocum temper got out of hand: "Don't get mad, son. Get even." And that was precisely what John Slocum intended to do at the first opportunity.

Miguel did not come to the cantina until well after midnight. He spoke to Juanito, then motioned Ortega and Slocum to come outside. He handed Ortega a folded piece of paper. Ortega read the telegraph message in light from a cantina window. For the next half minute Slocum waited anxiously, wondering what Tom said in the wire.

"What does it say?" he finally asked, when it seemed Ortega was taking too long to read only a few short lines.

"He agree to the price," Ortega replied gravely, "but he say you no bring money here. He say you come, take gold to village of Las Minas to pay for the woman. Las Minas is close to the river, maybeso too close for General Valdez to come."

"Ten thousand dollars in gold is a lot of money. If he wants the money, he'll come. If I remember right, Las Minas is south of the Rio Grande, maybe thirty or forty miles."

Ortega handed Slocum the paper. "This man say you must see woman is still alive," he added.

Slocum read the note quickly.

"John. Amount asked is agreed. You return at once. Take money to Las Minas prearranged time. Make sure Melissa is alive before you return. Las Minas is only acceptable meeting place. You set conditions. Signed Tom Spence."

"Anderson will pay the ten thousand," Slocum said,

wondering why Las Minas was Tom's suggestion. Was Tom helping Howard Anderson plan some sort of assurance that Melissa made it to the border? Hiring mercenaries? Why was Las Minas, an abandoned mining town southwest of Nuevo Laredo, the only acceptable meeting place?

Ortega took the message back. "Now we inform the general of what paper say. Maybeso the general will not come to Las Minas. If he say no, then woman will die, or he will keep her for his own woman."

"I reckon about all we can do is ask him," Slocum said in a voice as tired as he felt. "Means we have to ride back to Nava so I can see the girl, like the telegraph says, if General Valdez agrees to come to Las Minas."

Ortega still seemed troubled by the town's nearness to the border. "I do not think the general will go to Las Minas," he said. "Many Federales are in the north."

Juanito led them to the shed where their horses were tied. Ortega carried their bottle of tequila. Slocum was dreading another long ride back through the mountains to reach Nava. But one of his most important objectives was to be certain Melissa Anderson was alive and well before starting back to Laredo to arrange for the ransom.

Needing sleep, he mounted and reined out of the corral. A sky full of stars and a slice of new moon showed them the way to the outskirts of Saltillo.

Ortega was drunk, swaying in his saddle, holding onto the saddle horn to keep from falling off his horse when they rounded sharp turns climbing into the mountains. Juanito drank as much of the tequila as Ortega, but he seemed to show less effect as the night wore on. Passing the bottle back and forth, they drank and talked to each other in Spanish. Slocum watched the two men grow increasingly careless. Ortega's words soon became slurred. When they offered him the bottle, he pretended to drink from it. He sensed opportunity, yet even if he could free himself and get his guns back, he was no closer to rescuing Melissa than before. Valdez was still holding her prisoner. Nava was an armed camp. What good would it do to overpower these two men when Valdez and the girl were surrounded by guards with guns? He would be free to ride back to the safety of the border, while the girl remained in the same predicament.

Grudgingly, he accepted his fate. Until he talked to Valdez and made arrangements for her release, he was boxed in. There was nothing to do but wait until he met with Valdez. Attempting to do things peacefully was the only possible way to get Anderson's daughter back to Texas alive.

"Hey gringo!" Ortega cried, slumped in his saddle, weaving back and forth with the gait of his horse as they climbed a steep mountain trail with a perpendicular drop to his left. "Maybeso General Valdez will order you shot by a firing squad also!"

Juanito chuckled. "I will volunteer to shoot him. I do not like rich gringos from the north. It will be a good thing to see him die. *Verdad?*"

"*Sí*, it is the truth, Juanito," Ortega agreed. "A bullet is a good thing when it kills rich *Americanos.*"

Both men laughed. Slocum bit his lip and said nothing, for now content to let them have their fun at his expense. He was much too tired to argue with them, nor did he want to think about young Ramón Casillas dying in front of a firing squad any longer. Since learning of the boy's death, he'd been haunted by it, by his role in sending Ramón to an early grave.

"Why you no talk to us, gringo?" Ortega demanded, losing the grin on his face when Slocum didn't say anything.

"I'm tired," he said. "Maybe it's too much tequila. I sure could use a few hours of sleep."

Juanito's voice echoed off the side of a cliff as they rode up a steepening grade. "If I shoot you now, gringo, you sleep for long time . . . how you say . . . forever?"

Ortega drank deeply, smacking his lips, as their horses made a turn topping a rise. "Forever is long time, gringo. This boy you send to Nava is dead forever. Maybeso same happen to you."

Slocum's bad temper went out of control for an instant and before he could think about what he was doing, he rode up beside Ortega where the trail was narrow, a drop of hundreds of feet off one side of a mountain. Doubling his right fist, he swung a punch aimed for Ortega's jaw, and when it landed, he could hear the crack of bone and feel the shock of his blow all the way to his shoulder.

Ortega screamed, flinging his tequila bottle in the air when he made a futile grab for his saddle horn. Too late, his hands clawed empty air as he sailed off his horse into the black abyss at the bottom of the steep slope. While Ortega was falling, Slocum made a half turn and then a dive from his saddle toward Juanito as quickly as he could spring from his stirrups. His head struck Juanito in the belly. He heard the Mexican grunt when air rushed from his lungs. The two of them fell sideways, slamming into a slab of rock running up the mountain. Slocum made a grab for the pistol holstered at Juanito's waist, but when his fingers closed, his hand came up empty.

They crashed heavily to the ground, Slocum atop Juanito's chest. Juanito's horse bolted away, galloping up the mountainside. Slocum reached for the Mexican's windpipe, and in the same instant, something heavy thudded into his skull.

He felt himself falling to one side, stunned, unable to get his arms or legs to obey him. Momentarily paralyzed, he heard a piercing cry in the distance, then a dull thump when Ortega fell to the rocks at the base of the mountain. Horses galloped away, and a split second later, another clubbing blow struck his head.

He was reaching for the Bowie knife concealed in his boot as a curtain of darkness enveloped him.

18

Slocum awoke to find himself bound hand and foot, gagged, unable to move. At first, still groggy, he fought his restraints until he realized the futility of it. Strips of rawhide bound his legs and wrists. A foul-tasting rag had been stuffed into his mouth, tied there by a faded red bandanna. Slowly, his mind cleared and he remembered events before he was knocked unconscious. Juanito had been too quick despite half a bottle of tequila. When Slocum reached for the Mexican's gun, it must have already been swinging in an arc toward the back of his head. Now Slocum had two sore, swollen knots on his skull and what was worse, he probably faced a death sentence for trying to escape from Ortega and Juanito in the dark. Ortega had fallen to certain death off the side of the mountain when Slocum hit him. Valdez would believe in an eye for an eye. He'd ordered Ramón shot for no better reason than coming to Nava without an engraved invitation.

Slocum examined his surroundings. He was in a small room made of cut stones and mortar, windowless, a sliver of sunlight at the bottom of a heavy wood door. A dirt floor. No furniture or other objects. Was he in Nava? Had Juanito tied him over the back of his horse and taken him to Valdez?

Struggling, his head pounding, he managed to sit up with his knees bent. His wrists were tied in front of him rather than behind his back. Blood seeped from his skin where the bindings cut into his flesh.

Suddenly remembering the knife in his boot, his hopes fell when he discovered it was gone. Slowly, the hopelessness of his situation began to sink in. He was a prisoner, bound hand and foot, probably in Nava awaiting an order for his execution by a firing squad. They would kill him the same way they'd killed Ramón Casillas, no doubt. Unless he could talk his way out of this mess, he was most likely spending the last few hours of his lifetime now. He'd been in dozens of close scrapes in the last twenty-odd years, and he'd always found some way out just in the nick of time. But how could he get out of this?

Despair closed in on him. He had never been one to give up, yet this time, things looked hopeless. He'd fought his way out of plenty of tight spots, but there had been his weapons to rely on, his skill with firearms to equalize long odds when they stood against him. Even when he faced an enemy with nothing but his fists, he'd found a way to gain the upper hand. But now, with his hands and feet tied together, he was utterly defenseless and at the mercy of Victoriano Valdez.

I can't give up now, he thought. *I'll find a way to get my hands free . . . somehow.*

By inching backward a little at a time, he reached the back wall of his prison and rested against it. The greasy rag in his mouth was making him nauseous, but the knot in the bandanna was too tight and he couldn't loosen it. The effort to move backward to the wall made his head throb with pain. He found he was slightly dizzy. Resting, his mind raced to find some way to convince the bandit leader that he was worth more alive than dead. Without him, there would be no ransom money paid, but would

Valdez listen to logic? Or would he simply put him to death the way he had the boy?

Closing his eyes, Slocum considered every possibility, what he might say to Valdez to keep him from ordering a firing squad. If it were left up to Juanito, he was sure the lanky Mexican was looking forward to killing him.

Damn the luck, he thought, when he couldn't come up with an answer to his dilemma that stood much chance of working. Then, in a moment of reflection, he knew it wasn't luck that had done him in. He'd been careless going into his hotel room that day and this was the price to be paid for it.

He'd been dozing when he heard someone unlocking the door and suddenly, he came wide awake. Two Mexicans in broad sombreros entered his room. He recognized one immediately. Juanito looked down at him with pure hatred in his eyes. The other man was tall and muscular, young, hardly more than twenty, with a dark mustache and a clean-shaven chin.

Juanito walked over to Slocum, his boots making a grinding noise on the dirt floor. "*Idiota*," he snarled. "You will die for what you did, gringo, for killing Julio."

Slocum mouthed a denial, that he hadn't meant to kill Ortega when he struck him. The rag stuffed in his cheeks prevented his words from being heard by either man.

The younger Mexican walked slowly across the room. He stared at Slocum for a moment, then he drew back a booted foot and swung a vicious kick at Slocum's legs. The blow landed, glancing off his thigh, the result of poor aim.

"*Bastardo*!" the young man cried, grimacing.

Juanito laughed dryly. "When General Valdez returns from Hidalgo, he will order your execution, gringo. Mañana, you will die before a firing squad! The only reason I did not kill you last night was the gold. The general wants this gold you say you pay for the woman." He gave Slocum a haughty glare, turned, and started for the door. "Come, Pedro. Let the gringo think about the bullets tomorrow, if this is the wish of General Valdez."

The other man grinned. "*Sí*, Juanito. Mañana he dies. It will be good to see this gringo bastardo die." Pedro turned on his heel and followed Juanito out the door.

The door was locked, then boots sounded moving away. When Slocum tried to swallow, he found he couldn't with the rag in his mouth. He remembered something Juanito said, that Valdez was in a place called Hidalgo. Perhaps the general's absence would buy him more time to figure a way out of here.

He rested his head on the wall, working his tongue so that most of the rag was balled on one side of his mouth so he could swallow. His wrists were hurting where the rawhide strips were cutting him. Taking a deep breath, he looked closely at the knots binding his hands. It would be impossible to untie those pieces of green cowhide, yet he might be able to untie the cord around his ankles and at least free his feet so he could stand.

One important bit of information had come from Juanito, that Valdez wanted Howard Anderson's gold. With the ransom as bait, it might still be possible to talk sense to Valdez. Without Slocum to arrange the exchange, there would be no gold. Juanito seemed to understand this. All Slocum had to do was convince Valdez that no ransom would be paid unless he made the deal.

His fingers were numb as he went to work on the leather tied around his ankles. But the rawhide, still damp before curing, was impossible to budge. As wet cowhide dried it would contract, making his bindings even tighter. By morning his wrists would be bleeding profusely.

After a few more minutes of futile struggle with the rawhide, he gave up and rested his aching head against the stone wall. It was useless to try any longer.

His stomach growled with hunger. He couldn't recall when he last ate a square meal. He was growing weaker, feeling sleepy, although the pain in his head had begun to subside.

A key entered the lock. Slocum opened his eyes. A man came into the room carrying a tin plate. He placed it on the floor in easy reach, then he knelt down and spoke softly, barely above a whisper. "I am Pedro Morales." He untied the bandanna and took the rag from Slocum's mouth.

Slocum remembered him as the young man who accompanied Juanito a few hours earlier, the one who had kicked him. Somewhere in the back of his brain, he knew he should recognize the name, yet his mind was still fuzzy from dozing.

He glanced down to the plate. A pile of beans in some sort of sauce filled a tortilla. He muttered, "Thanks," and reached for his food, when Pedro spoke again.

"Ramón Casillas was my cousin."

Suddenly, Slocum was wide awake. "They told me Valdez had him shot by a firing squad," he said quietly, searching Pedro's face.

Pedro nodded. "For coming to Nava without sending a messenger first from El Agave cantina. Ramón rode straight to the village and that is forbidden by Victoriano. Someone must come from El Agave to ask permission to come to Nava. Ramón did not know this. Victoriano ordered Ramón's death, as example to any others who dare to come here."

"I'm sorry about your cousin. I liked the boy. He died because of me, because of what I asked him to do. His death is on my conscience."

Now Pedro glanced over his shoulder, making sure no

one was listening outside. "Tonight I will come for you, along with two of my amigos. We will let you out of this room and give you a fast horse. That is all I can do for you, señor, but if you ride quickly to the Rio Grande, Victoriano will not send anyone across and you will be safe."

Slocum felt immediate relief, although he wondered why Pedro and his friends would take such a chance. "I'll owe you my life, Pedro." He thought about Melissa. "The girl . . . I need to find out if she's okay, and where she's being kept."

"He keeps her upstairs at the cantina," Pedro whispered. "I know of no one who has seen her except Juanito. He guards her room at night and when Victoriano is away."

Slocum's mind raced. "If you let me out tonight and give me a couple of guns, what are my chances of getting her out of that room and out of Nava?"

Pedro frowned. "It would be very dangerous, señor. And you would have to kill Juanito, who is very fast with *la pistola*, and the noise from a gun would awaken the others."

Slocum felt his anger swell. He owed Juanito for a bump on his head. "I'd almost enjoy killing that son of a bitch. If I had my knife, I might get it done quietly so there wouldn't be any gunshots. If you could find my Bowie knife and my pistols, or any kind of gun, I might be able to get the girl out of that room and onto a horse before anybody is the wiser. We'd need two fast horses and some weapons, if we're to stand any chance of getting to the border ahead of Valdez and the men he'll send after me."

Pedro was worried. "Juanito will be a very hard man to kill with a knife or a gun, señor. He is *uno malo hombre*, a bad one."

"You leave that up to me. If you can get me my knife and my guns, or any good pistol and a rifle, along with two fast horses, I'll handle the rest."

Pedro said, "I will see what I can do. I will ask José to look for your knife and the *pistolas*. He is a guard at the door into the cantina where Victoriano keep woman. José may be able to let you inside tonight, if no one else is watching. Many of our *soldados* are away with Victoriano in Hidalgo and for this reason, Nava is quiet tonight. Tonight will be your only chance to escape, señor. Tomorrow Victoriano returns."

"I'm grateful for the offer of help. If you come to Laredo, I'll see to it that you and your friends are well paid. The girl has a father who'll be very generous if you help me get her out of here."

Again, Pedro looked to the open door. "We are growing tired of this revolution," he said. "We do not fight *los* Federales for the liberation of our people, as Victoriano promised. All we do is rob *los ricos*, many rich people, so Victoriano can be rich. There are some in his army who do not believe him any longer. We are not fighting for a revolution. We have become nothing more than *bandidos*."

Slocum leaned forward. "For whatever reasons, I'm grateful that you're willing to help me escape."

Pedro's face turned to stone. "I help you because of what Victoriano did to Ramón, señor." He stood up and dusted off his knees. "We will come late tonight when everyone is asleep. I will ask José to find your guns and the knife, if he knows where Juanito keeps them. If he is unable to find your weapons, I will bring whatever I can. I will tell Doroteo that you need two fast horses. One thing you can be sure of, señor. Victoriano will send many *soldados* after you. If they catch you, they will kill you."

"Ask José if there's a way I can get upstairs to the

room where they keep the girl. If I can, I aim to take her with me.''

Pedro closed the door and locked it without saying more. He walked away, leaving Slocum to his thoughts.

''I've got a fighting chance now,'' he told himself, reaching for the tortilla and beans, realizing that he was starving. With hope for an escape, his mind cleared.

He recalled that Ortega had been carrying his Colt Peacemaker and his belly-gun when a punch sent him over the cliff to his death. His rifle and shotgun were in a sling on Juanito's saddle as they rode the high trail to Nava. Killing Juanito silently in order to get the girl downstairs might prove to be tricky, but it was possible if things went just right.

If he got the girl out of Nava, there was still the difficult task of negotiating a dangerous trail out of the mountains in the dark. Then a long ride to Saltillo to pick up Tom's blue roan gelding, and finally, a horse race across the Mexican desert to the Rio Grande. On the surface it appeared to be an almost impossible escape to pull off. Everything, down to the very last detail, would have to work smoothly. Even then, he would be counting on a sizable amount of luck.

Eating the last of his tortilla and beans, he licked his fingers and thought about what he faced in the coming hours and days.

19

Judging by sunlight coming under the door, Slocum knew when night came to Nava. Now and then he heard noises, footsteps near the room where he was being kept, occasional sounds of horses off in the distance. After dark, it grew quiet. There was nothing to do but wait for Pedro and his friends while hoping nothing went wrong with their plans to set him free.

He felt somewhat better after his meager meal and with the rag removed from his mouth he suffered less, although his wrists ached and bled as the rawhide dried, tightening. He wished he'd asked Pedro to cut his bindings, but it was the sort of thing that might give Pedro's plan away, should someone else come to check on their prisoner. Thus Slocum was forced to sit with his knees bent, resting against a stone wall, awaiting a slim chance to make his escape. Everything depended on Pedro and his amigos, José and Doroteo.

He remembered Pedro's swift kick when he accompanied Juanito into the room, and now he understood why it had been a glancing blow, a deliberate effort on Pedro's part to seem angry toward a gringo prisoner. It was good acting on Pedro's part.

He dozed again, allowing himself badly needed sleep. If he managed to get away from Nava, there would be no opportunity for sleep until he reached the Rio Grande. Valdez's men would hound him all the way to the border.

He'd only been asleep a short time when he heard someone put a key into the lock. The door swung open. Light from a coal oil lantern spilled into the room, briefly hurting Slocum's eyes. He blinked, and then he recognized the man holding the lantern. An inner voice told him something had gone wrong.

Juanito swaggered over near the wall and put his lamp on the floor a few feet from Slocum. He slowly drew a revolver from his gun belt. A savage grin raised the corners of his mouth. "How does it feel, gringo, to know you will die very soon?"

"That ain't been decided yet," Slocum answered defiantly, as his temper heated up. "Your general wants that ten thousand in gold I can bring him. I don't figure he'll have me killed until he gets his hands on that money. He'll keep me alive because me and that girl are worth ten thousand dollars to him."

Juanito came a half step closer. "Someone else can trade the woman for the gold."

"Without me, there's no one who can tell the girl's father she's still alive. He won't send any money to Las Minas without hearing from me that she's okay." Slocum watched Juanito's gun carefully to see if he meant to use it. "General Valdez will be mighty unhappy if something happens to me so he can't collect the gold. If I was you, I'd be thinking about that."

Sudden anger wiped the grin off Juanito's face. He set his jaw, then he swung the barrel of his pistol, striking a vicious blow across Slocum's left cheek.

Slocum tried to duck away from the gun much too slowly, and when it struck him, his head was driven back against the wall. He tasted blood. His ears were ringing. Fearing another blow, he drew back as far as he could, hunkering down to make as small a target as possible.

"I should kill you now, telling the general you tried to get away," Juanito spat, his feet spread apart as if he meant to come at Slocum again.

Slocum ran his tongue over his teeth slowly to see if any were broken. Blood filled his mouth from a cut inside his cheek. He said nothing else, watching Juanito.

Finally, Juanito straightened and holstered his gun. He took the lantern and moved to the door. "You will die, gringo," he promised. "Maybe soon, or later, I will put a bullet through your heart." He closed the door and locked it.

Slocum listened to him walk away before he spat out a mouthful of blood. His eyelids narrowed. "Maybe you won't live long enough to get the chance, asshole," he whispered, clenching his teeth in quiet rage.

Nursing a sore cheek, he allowed his temper to cool. If he got the opportunity, he didn't want anger to get in the way of his plan for revenge.

Slocum had all but given up hope that Pedro and his friends were coming to let him out, figuring something had backfired. Then, noise alerted him that someone was close to the door. A key turned tumblers in the lock very softly, and light from the stars spilled through the doorway onto the floor.

A shadow crept toward him and for a moment Slocum feared it was Juanito, coming back to kill him with a knife. But when he heard Pedro's voice, he relaxed.

"Two horses are saddled." A knife blade went to work on his wrist bindings, then his ankles were freed. "Here is your knife. Your rifle and shotgun are with the horses. I give you my own *pistola* and bullets. Your guns fell into the arroyo with Julio Ortega.''

Slocum was handed his Bowie knife and a gun belt holding a Colt .44 and loops full of cartridges. He stood up and strapped on the gun before sheathing the knife in his boot. ''What about getting to the girl?'' he whispered. ''Will José let me go upstairs?''

Pedro hesitated. ''It will be very dangerous. Another guard is at the front, and Juanito is upstairs in front of the door to the room where she is kept.''

''I'll take the chance,'' he told Pedro, eyeing the man's big sombrero. ''Let me have your sombrero. In the dark I'll look the same as everybody else. All you've got to do is show me where the horses are tied, and then take me to the back door of that cantina so José will let me in. I'll do the rest. If I can, I aim to silence Juanito with this knife so nobody will hear any ruckus. But if that don't work, I'll have to shoot my way out of the building and make a run for the horses.''

''*Buenas suerte, señor*,'' Pedro said, wishing him good luck. ''Come. I will show you the horses, then we go to the door where José is guard.'' He took off his sombrero and gave it to Slocum.

Slocum touched Pedro's shoulder. ''Don't forget to come to Laredo as soon as you can. There's a sizable reward in this for you and your two amigos if me and the girl get back to Texas alive.''

''We will come, señor. While the others are chasing you, we will go northwest to Piedras Negras to cross the river. If all goes well, we will see you in Laredo.''

''Come to the city marshal's office. Ask for Tom Spence. He will know if we made it okay. Now, show me those horses.'' With the sombrero covering most of his face, he followed Pedro to the doorway and peered out.

''This way,'' Pedro whispered, motioning Slocum down a narrow road lined with small adobe houses.

They left quietly, walking on the balls of their feet while keeping to the darkest shadows.

José was short, scarcely five feet tall. He stood beside a rear door into the two-story building where Slocum was taken when he first came to Nava. As Pedro led Slocum down a dark alley to the back of the cantina, José beckoned to them. He held a finger to his lips and whispered, "*Silencio.*"

Slocum saw José's serape and had an idea. "Give me this, so I will look like the others," he whispered.

José nodded and slipped the serape over his head.

Slocum took off the sombrero and put José's serape over his shoulders. With the sombrero on his head, his shadow looked like those of the natives in Nava. He'd been shown to a small stable where a big black gelding and a smaller chestnut were saddled and tied. He knew the route he would take when he made his run to reach the horses.

He drew his Bowie knife from his boot and concealed it under the serape, after checking the loads in the .44 Pedro gave him. A moment passed. He took a deep breath and carefully opened the door without saying a word, his senses keened, his heart racing. José and Pedro slipped away quietly into the dark as Slocum crept into the building.

The cantina was empty. Moving as softly as his bulk would allow, he tiptoed over to a set of stairs leading to the second floor. Being careful not to make a noise, he started up each of the steps after testing them for a sound that might give him away to anyone upstairs.

He crept to the top of a darkened hallway where he waited for his eyes to adjust to poor light. A window at the end of the hall admitted a pale glow from stars in a clear night sky. There, in front of a door, Slocum saw an outline, a figure slumped in a chair against one wall.

Moving as softly as he could, he inched down the hall with his knife hidden beneath José's serape. As he got closer to the figure, he saw more detail. Juanito was asleep, his head lolled to one side, his sombrero resting on the floor beside him. But as Slocum came closer, suddenly a floorboard creaked underneath his boot.

Juanito jerked, turning his head in Slocum's direction. For a few precious seconds he did not move while Slocum came toward him.

"*Quien es?*" Juanito asked, still seated in his chair, not expecting trouble.

"Juan," Slocum answered softly, walking faster, only a few yards from Juanito now.

"*Quien?*" Juanito asked again, hearing an unfamiliar voice.

Slocum reached the chair just as Juanito sprang suddenly to his feet. Sweeping the serape aside, Slocum grinned savagely. "I am Juan," he snarled. "John is my name in English."

Juanito clawed for his pistol. Slocum sent the blade of his Bowie into the Mexican's breastbone with the force of a kick from a mule. Cartilage snapped like dry kindling when the tip of the knife pierced Juanito's ribs, while at the same time Slocum made a grab for the Mexican's gun with his free hand, keeping it from leaving its holster. As he drove his blade all the way to its hilt, he lifted the brim of Pedro's sombrero so Juanito got a good look at his face in the starlight.

Air rushed from Juanito's lungs, and he was driven back against the wall, pinioned there, his eyes bulging with pain and fear as Slocum's knife entered his heart.

"Die quietly, you rotten son of a bitch!" Slocum hissed, his face only inches from Juanito's.

"How?" Juanito gasped.

Slocum twisted his knife, doing as much damage as he could, hearing bone and gristle pop inside the Mexican's chest when the heavy blade turned between broken ribs. Blood showered over his hand, the knife handle, dribbling to the floor like rain from a leaking roof.

He jerked the knife free, letting Juanito's body slide down the wall to the floor with a thump. Slocum took both pistols from Juanito's gun belt and stuck them in the waistband of his denims. Air bubbled from the dying Mexican's mouth while Slocum tried to open the door. He found the door locked and threw his shoulder against it, splintering the door frame on his first try.

He saw a woman bolt upright on a bed across the room. To calm her fears he said softly, "Don't worry, Melissa. I'm from Texas. Your father sent me. Get dressed and we're getting out of here as quick as we can."

The woman, wearing a nightgown, didn't move. Starlight from a window showed him the surprised expression on her face.

"Get dressed!" he commanded. "We're running out of time!"

As though she suddenly realized what was happening, the girl leapt from her bed to don a pair of pants draped over a chair in one corner of the bedroom.

Slocum hurried over to her. "No time for anything else," he said. "My name is John Slocum, and tonight you and I are in for the ride of our lives. Follow me." He took her by the arm and led her into the hallway.

When Melissa saw the body and smelled blood pooled near the door, she drew in a quick breath, but before she had time to utter a word, Slocum was pulling her toward the stairs.

They hurried down the steps two at a time and turned for the back door. Sheathing his bloody Bowie knife, Slocum drew one of his pistols before he tugged Melissa into the alley.

"Run," he said, taking her by the arm. "We've got a couple of horses waiting for us. I sure as hell hope you can ride."

"I can ride as well as any man," Melissa replied, and by the tone of her voice, he knew she meant it.

They ran east down a darkened alleyway, toward the little stable. The girl was barefoot and at times she stumbled over something unseen in the inky blackness. Covering their progress with a pistol, Slocum ran as fast as Melissa could travel, his heart pounding. If they could make it through the gates out of Nava without being discovered, they stood a fighting chance of making it back to the border alive.

He was gasping for air by the time they reached the stable. Doroteo, an elderly Mexican with a gray beard, swung open a gate and stood back as they mounted the horses. Slocum chose the black, giving Melissa the chestnut. Wheeling his gelding, Slocum led the way out of the barn, turning south.

They galloped down empty streets, awakening the village dogs with the sound of pounding hooves. Melissa rode beside him, resting easily in the seat of her saddle as though she'd been born on the back of a horse.

Racing toward the gate out of Nava, Slocum saw a sleeping guard near the opening toss his blanket aside to sit up in his bedroll, staring at the pair of galloping horses. He and Melissa raced through the gap in the stone wall at full speed, leaning over their horses' necks.

Not a shot was fired when they rode away from the village, but Slocum knew their run for freedom had only just begun. He looked over his shoulder. Lanterns all over Nava were springing to life and he could hear angry shouts above the rattle of iron horseshoes.

20

Guided by starlight and glow from a sliver of new moon, they raced their horses to the first steep descent where the trail to Saltillo started down from higher altitudes in the Sierra Madres. Their horses were winded by the time they reached a drop where it was too steep to hold a gallop. Slocum reined down to a trot and let his horse choose its own footing in spots where loose rocks made the trail dangerous. Melissa rode close behind him, holding a tight rein on her chestnut. As soon as they were out of sight from Nava, he turned in the saddle and spoke to her.

"Are you okay?" he asked, seeing dark places that could be bruises on her face.

"I'm okay," she answered, tight-voiced. "I've got a hundred questions, but they can wait."

Slocum's black stumbled over a rock, caught itself, and held a steady trot down a twisting pathway into a stand of tall pines. Once they reached those trees, it would be much harder for a man with a rifle to take a potshot at them and maybe get lucky. "I can tell you a few things," he continued, twisting back and forth to see what lay ahead as well as any sign of pursuit from behind. "We've got one hell of a long ride to reach the border. We'll be chased by Valdez's men and dodging Federales. The only thing we have to fear from Federales is that they'll detain us, asking us questions as to why we're here and how we got here. I suspect Valdez has informants with the Federales and if we're found by the wrong bunch of Mexican soldiers, somebody might get word to Valdez. Our biggest worry is being run down from the rear by a bunch of Valdez's men. They've got good horses now because your father raised some of the best, like the ones we're riding now. It's gonna be a horse race to the Rio Grande, and whoever can stay in the saddle longer stands the best chance to win.''

"I can ride as long as it takes," Melissa said, edging her horse alongside Slocum's where a wide spot in the trail gave them room. "Don't make any allowances for me because I'm a woman. I can outride most of my dad's cowhands. He'd tell you that if he was here."

He got a close look at her for the first time as she rode beside him. She was a beautiful girl with long blond hair, and her face was an almost perfect oval. Her nightdress was open at the neck, revealing the cleft of her small, rounded breasts. "I don't doubt you can ride, Melissa, but this is gonna be a test of endurance for us and these horses. There's a spare horse belongs to Tom Spence at the livery in Saltillo, and I aim to stop and get it, just in case one of these horses goes lame on us or runs out of wind. If we have a spare horse, our odds are better of making it."

"Like I said, Mr. Slocum, don't show me any favors because I'm a woman. I can stay in a saddle as long as any man, and you won't hear me complain." She glanced over her shoulder, and as she spoke again, there was fear in her voice. "I won't go back to them, no matter what. I'd let them kill me, before I'd go back."

They entered the pines and struck a lope again. Slocum

leaned out of the saddle so she could hear him above the rumble of hooves, intending to comfort her as much as he could. "Call me John, Melissa. And don't worry about them taking you back. I'm a right decent shot with a rifle or a handgun, if I do say so myself. If any of them get too close, I'll prove it. Just so long as our horses hold up, I'll nearly guarantee you I'll get you back to your father's ranch."

She was looking at him closely, riding so their knees almost touched. "You killed that awful Juanito, didn't you?" she asked.

He didn't answer her, thinking it should be obvious.

"Are you a professional killer hired by my dad?" she persisted, when she got no reply to her first question.

"I wouldn't call myself a killer. I'm a detective for some of the railroads, mostly. There've been occasions when I've been asked to use my guns. Your father hired me to see if there was a way to negotiate your release. He was willing to pay ten thousand in gold to get you back, but before things could be arranged properly, I got crossways with one of Valdez's men."

"Did you kill him, too?"

Slocum didn't like the way a straight answer would sound, so he put it a little differently. "He fell after I hit him in the jaw. The fall was a bit longer than either of us figured. I was told the fall killed him. That's when they locked me up, until Valdez decided what to do with me. It's a long story, about how I got out. We had help from some of Valdez's soldiers."

Another sharp drop in the trail presented itself, ending any chance of conversation until they reached the bottom of a narrow gorge, the gorge where Ortega had fallen to his death. There was no point in telling the girl about it now.

The black gelding was rough-gaited but dependable

enough, and it had stamina, like the other Anderson horses Slocum had seen. A time or two the black lost its footing in the dark, but overall it seemed to be a seasoned ranch horse with good speed. Melissa's chestnut appeared to have one serious flaw—it was short in its stride at a run, making it a sure loser in a horse race. He meant to get Tom's blue roan from that stable if he could, if no one had stolen it while he was held prisoner in Nava.

They faced other serious problems. All his money had been taken while he was unconscious. And his food, along with the rest of his belongings, was back in the hotel room in Saltillo. Without money they couldn't buy anything to eat, and it would be far too time consuming and risky to ride to the hotel to get his saddlebags and bedroll.

We'll manage somehow, he thought, keeping his concerns to himself. No sense worrying the girl.

At the bottom of the trail, they urged their horses to a gallop across a flat leading to the next ridge where the path dropped again. As they crossed the flat, Slocum looked behind them, and what he saw at the top of the trail made his blood run cold. Horsemen began the descent, outlined against a night sky made bright by winking stars. He quickly counted more than a dozen riders, then still more mounted men came spilling over the rimrock above the gorge.

"Here they come!" he cried to Melissa.

The slender girl whirled around in her saddle, then she took the ends of her reins and began whipping her tiring chestnut on its shoulders, forcing the animal to run harder than ever.

Dawn had come to Saltillo by the time they got to the stable where he left Tom's roan. Their horses were exhausted, panting, necks and shoulders covered with lather after a hard push out of the mountains ahead of Valdez's men. The city was still asleep in the early morning hours and the roads they traveled were empty of all but a few goat herders and an occasional vaquero. As soon as they reached the livery, Slocum motioned for the girl to stay back while he rode to the barn looking for the roan.

He found an unexpected piece of luck when he saw the gelding in a stall. The liveryman was nowhere in sight. Slocum jumped to the ground and took a sisal rope halter from a wood peg on the stable wall, haltering the roan as quickly as he could, fearing the old man might show up demanding money for the horse's keep, money Slocum didn't have.

He led the horse out of its stall and swung up on his black with the lead rope dallied around his saddle horn. In less than half a minute, he was riding away from the livery with his spare horse, beckoning for Melissa to follow him toward a piñon forest that would take them around the city without being seen.

"We got lucky," he told her, leading the way into slender pines along a goat trail. "Your horse is done in. Soon as we find a secluded spot, we'll change your saddle to this blue. He can run. That chestnut can't go much farther with a rider if we keep pushing like this."

Melissa was watching their back trail. "I don't see them any more," she said.

Slocum knew what to expect. "They'll be coming. You can be sure we'll see 'em again before long."

In a clearing among the pines, they halted long enough to put the girl's saddle on Tom's roan. He haltered the chestnut and swung aboard his black, tying off the lead rope so he was leading the extra horse. Moments later, they were off at a gallop around Saltillo, staying hidden in piñons wherever they could.

A warm sun brightened the mountain valley. When they left the mountains, they would encounter blistering desert heat. He knew their horses would suffer, yet there was no choice. Not far behind them, Valdez's men were conducting a manhunt. If he and the girl were found, the outcome would be certain. He also made a grim discovery, thinking about a time when he needed his rifle. There were no spare cartridges. Seven shells were in the tube, and two shells in the shotgun's chambers. The rest of the ammunition he had was in belt loops for the .44 he carried. If it came down to a gunfight, he had precious few bullets to shoot at long range, and a close-quarters fight would endanger the girl with lead flying from all directions.

They found the wagon road to Monterrey. Here there was a danger of running into Federale patrols. However, the presence of Federales would also keep Valdez's men at a safe distance. In either case, Slocum knew he was headed into the toughest part of getting Melissa back to Texas. He hoped he wouldn't have to fight his way across northern Mexico to get it done.

On the road to Monterrey, travelers sometimes gave Melissa odd looks when they noticed her nightshirt. Cart and wagon traffic was heavy in places, slow-moving caravans of freighters and some burro carts full of produce and pottery. Slocum kept a sharp eye out for soldiers in the distance while holding a steady trot in spite of the afternoon heat. They were in gently rolling desert hills to the southwest of Monterrey, entering dry brushland that would stretch all the way to the Texas border. Water would be as scarce as before, and they had no canteens. Continually looking over his shoulder, he watched for pursuing horsemen. For now, it was clear behind them.

As the day wore on, Melissa talked to him more. She had dark purple bruises on her cheeks and her bottom lip was swollen. But she sat her horse with determination and never once complained of the heat, although when she turned backward in the saddle, he saw a trace of fear on her face.

"I'm so grateful you came," she told him once as they topped a low hill overlooking the outskirts of Monterrey. "I was numb to what he was doing to me . . . it was like a bad dream, a nightmare that wouldn't end."

"It's over," he promised, not quite as sure of it as he made it sound. If Valdez's men caught up to them in open country, it would be a one-sided fight with only seven shells for his rifle.

Melissa was frowning at him. "You're just one man. He can send fifty men to track us down."

He grinned, more to give her confidence than any humor he saw in their present situation. "It's like a big game of chess. If we make the right moves, they can't corner us. But if they do manage to find us, a little sharpshooting will slow them down a bit, long enough for us to get to the Rio Grande."

For the first time, she smiled. "Are you as brave as you sound, John Slocum?"

He touched the brim of Pedro's sombrero in a mock salute. "Yes ma'am, I am. And I'm a damned decent shot, too. Sounds like a touch of bragging, maybe, but if they get too close, I'll prove it to you."

Her smile faded as her expression changed. "You're a very handsome man. I'll bet you're quite a hand with the ladies."

"I get by," he told her, avoiding the look she gave him.

Trotting their horses off the hilltop, Slocum saw open land running west of the city. "Let's get off this road. There's a bigger chance we'll encounter Federales close to Monterrey and I'll feel better if we stay wide of town."

He swung off the wagon ruts and headed into empty prairie. The sun-baked ground was hard, difficult to travel dodging beds of cactus and thick brush bristling with thorns. In the back of his mind this was a way to throw off their pursuers, cutting a few miles from the distance they would have to travel to get to the road to Sabinas Hidalgo and Nuevo Laredo.

Heat waves danced from bald spots in the caliche lying in their wake. Their horses were sweating. The little chestnut was rested now, but still having difficulty staying up with the bigger horses capable of much longer strides. Melissa rode up beside Slocum, her bare feet barely able to touch her stirrups.

"I'll be so happy to see my dad again, and the ranch. But it will be a sad homecoming, too. Several of dad's best cowboys were killed or wounded when those bandits attacked the ranch."

Slocum decided it was time to give her the truth. "All of them are dead, Melissa. Your father told me he lost every man he had that day, trying to defend the place."

"All of them?" she asked, sounding as if she were about to cry.

"Sorry to be the one to tell you . . ."

Tears formed in the corners of her eyes. To save her from any embarrassment, he looked away, casting a glance over the land behind them.

His gaze wandered to a tiny dust cloud on the horizon. He squinted to help keep out the sun's fierce glare. For a moment, he watched the dust rise from the prairie.

"They've found us," he declared, when he could make out men on horses below the cloud of caliche. He reached for his rifle and drew it out, levering a cartridge into the chamber, letting the hammer down gently with his thumb. "One of them's a pretty good tracker," he added. "They found our tracks where we left the main road a few miles back.''

Melissa was frozen to her saddle watching dust boil up from the desert. ''Dear God,'' she whispered. ''I hope you're as good with a gun as you claim to be.''

21

Where the land allowed it, Slocum stayed off the skyline to keep from being too easily seen by Valdez's men. He hoped for a chance to slow them down where their tracks would be harder to find across sun-baked ground. Down in his gut, he knew those men were as certain of their direction as he was: north, to the Texas border, and safety for himself and the girl.

He glanced up at the sun. Four or five hours of daylight remained. After dark, pursuit would come more slowly. Whoever was reading their tracks so skillfully would, of necessity, take more time getting it done. Slocum knew he was faced with a very dangerous gamble after sunset; ride open country where travel was slower yet they would be harder to find, or strike the main road north of Monterrey that led to Laredo where there were no obstacles, nothing to slow a horse down, merely mile after mile of roadway through the desert. It would be far more dangerous to ride through the brush, giving Valdez's men time to send riders ahead along the main road to cut them off. But sticking to the brushlands offered less risk of an all-out gun battle. First, the Mexicans would have to find them before any shooting started. The desert offered countless places to hide, but no water for themselves or their horses. A choice had to be made when the sun went down and a bad guess could cost them their lives.

Trotting their mounts, galloping now and then, they pushed steadily northward, angling for the Laredo road. And always, on the horizon behind them, the cloud of dust crept closer.

"I don't see how they can be gaining on us," Slocum said, when they crossed a brushy knob with a better view to the south. "It don't make any sense."

Melissa watched the dust and tiny specks beneath it. Her complexion had turned white, making her bruises more evident on her cheeks. She shaded her eyes from the sun with a small hand. "It almost looks like some of those horses don't have riders," she said, "only I can't be sure at this distance."

Slocum stood in his stirrups, squinting into the heat haze to see the dark spots below the ever-present caliche cloud. "I think that's the answer," he said, trying to keep the pronouncement from sounding too grim. "They brought spare horses. They must be changing mounts every few miles. Smart. Whoever called that shot knows how to cross a desert in a hurry."

"They're going to catch up to us, aren't they?" she asked, as if she already knew the answer.

Slocum hurried his black off the knob, down a winding ravine so shallow it was barely noticable as a dry wash until they rode directly into it. "If they do, little lady, they'll get a taste of lead. It'll be dark soon. Then some of the advantages take a turn our way. If I can find the right place to make a stand, I can pick a few of 'em off. It'll slow them down when I start to kill a few of 'em. They won't be coming so all-fired fast when I toss a few bullets their way."

Melissa was looking at the pistols he'd taken from

Juanito that were stuck in the waistband of his pants. "I can shoot," she said. "Dad taught me how to shoot when I was real young. If you'll give me one of those guns, I can help some if they get in pistol range."

He admired her spunk and told her so. "You're tougher than I imagined you'd be, Melissa. You ride like a Comanche, so if you say you can shoot, I believe you." He handed her one of the .44s. "Don't waste any shells. We aren't exactly overloaded with ammunition."

Looping her reins around her saddle horn, she opened the .44's loading gate expertly and inspected the brass cartridge caps by rolling the cylinder with her thumb. Without saying a word, she tucked the revolver into the top of her pants and hid it beneath her nightgown.

Riding the ravine at a gallop, they continued north as fast as weary horses could travel.

Behind a rocky outcrop, hidden by darkness and a crown of yucca plants growing around the top of the ledge, Slocum raised his Winchester to his shoulder, being careful to keep the barrel from reflecting starlight by holding it in a shadow cast by a fan of spiked yucca leaves. A line of riders came down a creek bed single file, following its dry bottom. One rider leaned out of his saddle, reading their hoofprints in the sand. This was the man Slocum planned to execute, the expert tracker who guided the others so unerringly, no matter how hard Slocum tried to throw off pursuit by crossing hard ground.

Melissa waited behind the outcrop, holding their horses, with instructions to keep them from nickering at all costs. Surprise was the key element Slocum needed to slow down Valdez's men in the dark. When they found out he'd stopped running and was ready to fight, they would be more cautious. He figured he could drop a few of the front riders before they scattered to find cover, and by then he and Melissa would be moving north again.

Waiting, sighting in on the tracker's chest, he silenced the voice of his conscience for what he was about to do. Shooting an unsuspecting man for any reason, ambushing him without warning, was something he'd only done in wartime. But in many respects, this was a war and he closed his mind to what he was about to do. Killing some of these men was necessary in order to have a chance to get the girl back to Texas.

When the range was right, when he knew he could not miss, he gently nudged the rifle's trigger. A thundering report ended the desert silence. The Winchester slammed into his shoulder, yellow flame spitting from its barrel as the explosion echoed across the brushlands surrounding the dry stream. The tracker jerked in his saddle, emitting a piercing scream when he was torn from the back of his plunging, rearing horse.

Slocum levered another shell, swinging his gun sights to a man aboard a pinto. With fractions of a second to get his aim, he squeezed off a second shot, wincing when the roar of his gun came so close to his right ear. A Mexican toppled from the pinto with his arms windmilling, as though he meant to fly. His horse made a lunge and the rider fell on his back without uttering a cry while his pinto galloped away.

Quickly ejecting the spent cartridge, Slocum readied a third shell and found a target among half a dozen more dark shapes that were racing away from the gunfire. Steadying his sights, he made sure of his shot before pulling the trigger again. A heavy rider wearing a straw sombrero and bandoliers stiffened when Slocum's bullet struck him in the ribs. He went spinning off his horse, spread-eagled, crashing to the creek bed on his belly, skidding to a halt near an ocotillo stalk.

Slocum almost took a fourth shot at a speeding rider

before he lowered his rifle. The man was too far away to be sure of a hit, and ammunition for his Winchester was too precious to waste. He crawled backward and stood up, trotting down the back side of the outcrop with the scent of burnt gunpowder filling his nose.

"Let's get out of here," he told Melissa, swinging aboard the black.

They were off at a steady lope through an opening in tight tangles of thorny brush, riding northeast to strike the road to Laredo. Slocum made a decision earlier that night—to make this a horse race after he gave Valdez's men a little taste of hot lead. Too much time had been wasted winding through cactus and mesquite, giving the Mexicans time to get ahead of them if some had split off to take the Laredo road.

Melissa rode up alongside him where a wide spot in the brush gave her room. "How many did you shoot?" she asked in a voice he barely heard above the rattle of shod hooves. "You fired three times."

"I dropped three of them," he answered quietly, not wanting to think about the way he'd done it from ambush. "I got the man who was reading our tracks. Maybe it'll slow 'em down a bit if they lost their tracker."

She cast a quick look over her shoulder. Although she did not say anything about his marksmanship, her silence was enough to convince him that she wouldn't have any more questions about his aim.

He thought about the men he'd killed. Shooting them from ambush wasn't his style, but under the circumstances, he'd had no real choice.

The road was empty, a pale white line stretching across mile after mile of desert, illuminated by stars and a piece of moon. A coyote barked off in the distance. Night birds whistled to each other from mesquite limbs on either side of the ruts. For several hours they had the road to themselves. Slocum rode the chestnut now, giving his black gelding a rest. The little horse was game but too short-coupled to carry him without tiring easily at much of a pace. Tom's big blue roan handled the girl's weight without effort. All three horses were gaunt-flanked from lack of water after so many punishing miles through desert heat. Slocum's lips were dry, cracking, and he knew the girl was suffering, too. To her credit, she made no complaint whatsoever, riding beside him at a trot as casually as if they were in no danger at all.

"Whatever my dad's paying you to do this, it won't be enough to make up for what you've done," she said, after several minutes of silence. "You've got a lot of guts, John Slocum, more than any man I ever met. You haven't told me much about yourself, only that you're a detective for a railroad."

"There ain't all that much to tell, really. I'm on the move quite a bit. Never was inclined to stay in one place very long."

"I suppose that means you don't have a wife."

"No wife. Never found a woman who could tolerate me for all that long, I reckon."

"No regular girlfriends?"

"Not so you'd notice. I've got a few lady friends I see from time to time, but nothing you'd call regular."

After a moment, Melissa asked, "Have you ever wanted to stay with a woman you loved?"

He glanced up at the sky, thinking about an honest answer to her question. "It's fair to say I've loved a good share of women in my time, but I get this dose of wanderlust pretty often. I get an itch to see what's on the other side of the mountain, so to speak. Some men aren't built to stay in the same place. I reckon I'm part of that breed."

"Boys my age are mostly a bunch of fools," she said.

"They act silly as a goose when a woman looks them in the eye. I can't stand foolish-acting men. My dad says I'm too particular when it comes to boys."

He didn't offer an opinion on that subject. Melissa was a girl older than her years, it seemed, but right now he faced more pressing matters than a girl's tastes in men. Getting out of this part of Mexico alive promised to be more of a chore than he first figured.

Later, off in the distance, he spied a small adobe hut west of the road. A few taller mesquites grew in clusters near the house. "There'll be water at that adobe," he said, thinking out loud. "Maybe whoever lives there won't mind giving us some for our horses. How's your Spanish?"

"I was born close to the Mexican border. I speak enough to ask for water."

"Some folks down here don't like Americans all that much. I hope these are friendly. It's late, close to midnight. We could get shot at."

They rode to a narrow lane running to the house. As soon as they turned down the lane, a dog began to bark near the adobe. A moment later, a lantern flickered to life behind one of the windows. Slocum kept his right hand near the butt of Pedro's gun as they approached the front of the hut.

They stopped twenty yards from the house. A bare-chested man holding a lantern peered around his door frame. The dog stopped barking.

"*Por favor, señor,*" Melissa began, "*nosotros carencia agua.*"

For several seconds the man said nothing, then he pointed to a well beside his house. "*Como no, señorita,*" he replied.

"We can have water," Melissa told Slocum, swinging

down from her saddle. Then she spoke to the Mexican. *"Muchas gracias, señor."*

Slocum got down and went to the well, finding a bucket on a piece of rope. He sent the bucket down, casting a wary look back along the road by which they had come, finding it empty.

Maybe we'll make it after all, he thought, giving water to each of their horses. Shooting those three men appeared to have given them a considerable lead.

Looking north, he knew they weren't far from Sabinas Hidalgo. They faced another brutal stretch of desert to the border, miles of dry road and killing heat that would take a terrible toll on their horses. Remembering the distance, Slocum decided it was too soon to think they could make it ahead of experienced Mexicans who knew this country.

After drinking himself and giving Melissa all the water she wanted, he changed his saddle to the black. He wanted them to be as ready as possible for a horse race.

They rode away from the little hut, after Melissa thanked the owner again for giving them water. Back on the main road to Sabinas Hidalgo, they turned north. Beneath a velvety night sky, they struck a steady trot, having the road to themselves.

Much later, when his eyelids had grown heavy, they passed through Sabinas Hidalgo while the village was asleep. Slocum kept thinking how peaceful things seemed since he fired those three shots from the rocks. Was it possible that shooting a few of Valdez's men had been enough to turn them back?

A little voice inside his head told him how foolish this notion was. More of a feeling than anything else, he sensed trouble was close at their heels, getting closer with each passing hour.

22

Melissa's bare face and arms were blistered red by the sun, despite the fact Slocum had given her Pedro's sombrero. A day of riding hard through the heat put more miles behind them than he figured. Passing the road leading to Rancho Bustamante had reminded him of Ramón last night, but nothing could be changed, and he put it from his thoughts. All day, keeping a close watch over their back trail, they saw nothing but travelers and freight wagons and donkey carts bound for Laredo or Monterrey. It seemed the men dogging their tracks had given up.

Passing through the tiny village of La Gloria as dark fell on the prairie, Slocum found himself filled with more hope. He was still nagged by the feeling that someone was back there, but no matter how closely he studied the southern horizon, he found nothing amiss, no large groups of horsemen.

Night brought an immediate cooling to the desert. At La Gloria they had watered their animals and drank themselves from a water trough in front of a small market. Because he and the girl were starving, he traded one of Juanito's Colt pistols for a bundle of corn tortillas, dried sausages, and a goatskin water bag which they filled at the trough. They'd eaten like starved wolves, drank again, and ridden on. Slocum wasn't too worried now, being without one handgun. He still had four shells in the Winchester, two loads in his shotgun, and plenty of cartridges in his belt loops for Pedro's revolver and the one Melissa carried. By the look of things behind them, their race to the border might have ended at the dry creek where he shot three of their pursuers from ambush. Valdez's men had been easier to discourage than he guessed.

As darkness crept over the brushlands, he fought a need for sleep. By morning, if he could stay awake in his saddle, they should be within sight of the Rio Grande. Their worn-down horses held a steady trot into the darkening night and soon they had the roadway to themselves.

It was the girl who first alerted him to the danger. She gasped and cried out, "Those men! Who are they?"

Five Mexicans in dust-caked sombreros sat lathered horses in the middle of the road ahead of them. Slocum blinked and came wide awake suddenly, straightening in the saddle. He knew by the rifles the men carried, resting the butt plates atop their thighs so as to be ready to use them, that these were men from Valdez who had somehow gotten around them by another route.

Melissa squinted into slanting morning sunlight. "See that big one!" she exclaimed, pointing to a heavyset Mexican on a big yellow dun. Tears choked her voice when she added, "That's him! That's Victoriano Valdez!"

Half a mile separated them from the men blocking the roadway and he asked, "How can you be so sure when they're so far away?"

"I'll never forget what he looks like—after what he did to me. That's him, the one riding the tall buckskin." She looked over at Slocum then, and tears welled in her eyes. "He can kill me, but he won't take me back. I'd rather die fighting him than be tied to his bed again!'' She drew Juanito's Colt from under her nightdress with a shaky hand and thumbed the hammer back to a cocked position.

"Take it easy," Slocum warned, reaching for his Winchester. He gave the men a closer examination. "I'm gonna turn the little chestnut loose so it won't slow us down. You swing that roan so you're riding directly behind me. Only one way to do this, and that's ride right at 'em, reining back and forth from one side of this road to the other. A moving target is mighty damn hard to hit. Soon as I've emptied this rifle, we hold our fire until we know we're in pistol range. Make every shot count. Don't shoot until you're sure of your target. If it's a fight they want, I'm damn sure ready to oblige 'em, only it don't make sense to waste a shot. Hold your fire as long as you can and lean over that horse's neck so they won't have much to aim at. If they shoot one of our horses, we'll ride double the rest of the way. By my rough guess, the river ain't all that far.''

The girl was staring at the five riders. She sleeved tears from her cheeks and nodded. "I'll be right behind you," she told him. "Don't worry about me. I'll be okay."

He readied the Winchester, cocking it, then he released the lead rope to the chestnut gelding. "Let's ride, little lady, and don't make a shot until you know you can't miss. Keep as low on that horse's neck as you can and stay behind me."

Heeling his black forward, he started toward Valdez and his gunmen, judging the distance he would need before he had a chance to drop one from the saddle with a rifle shot. With just four cartridges in the Winchester, he couldn't afford to waste a single shot. When he got in range, he would have to halt the black just long enough to steady his aim.

He urged the black horse to a lope. When the five men saw him charging toward them, they held a hurried conversation. The one Melissa identified as Victoriano was the first to send his horse to a gallop, riding straight for Slocum and Melissa. They were on a collision course, those five men and Slocum. He was reminded of Second Bull Run during the war, when Rebel officers ordered cavalrymen into the teeth of Union gun emplacements, a slaughter for those Confederates who charged wooded hills full of cannon and muskets.

The drumming of the black's hooves beat out a rhythm while he raced toward Victoriano and his men. Slitting his eyes to keep out the sun's glare, Slocum measured distance, calculating the moment when he would pull his horse to a halt. If his aim was true, he meant to unseat Victoriano first, a lesson from the Indian wars in Wyoming when a chief fell from his horse. Losing a leader sometimes broke the spirit of the Cheyennes, taking them out of a fight.

At four hundred yards, the range was still too great and he forced himself to keep moving ahead, although a knot of fear was beginning in his belly. He began reining back and forth from one wagon rut to the other in hopes of throwing off aim from any of Valdez's men. Slocum could see Valdez riding out in front of his *pistoleros* as a brave leader should. "Just stay there where I can see you," he muttered to himself, drumming his heels into the black's ribs.

When he judged they were less than three hundred yards apart, Slocum jerked back on his reins, bringing his horse to a sliding stop in the middle of the road. With the Winchester clamped to his shoulder, he drew a bead on Victoriano's chest, waiting for the exhausted black horse to settle, holding still. Then, for an instant, his rifle sights rested on Valdez. Valdez kept riding, galloping closer.

Slocum raised his gun sights to allow for the distance and pulled the trigger.

The explosion spooked his horse, almost pitching Slocum from the saddle until he grabbed his saddle horn. But as he did so, he kept watching Victoriano, levering another shell into place. For a moment, he was sure he'd missed badly—Valdez continued toward him at full speed aboard his racing dun. Then, as if he'd run up against an invisible length of rope stretched across the road, Victoriano flew off the rump of his horse, flinging his rifle in the air, his sombrero floating above his head spinning like a child's top.

Valdez landed on his neck and shoulders, skittering across a dusty wagon rut while his buckskin veered off the road through a wall of mesquite and cholla spines. Valdez landed limply, arms and legs askew, and by the way he fell, Slocum knew he was dead. In the same span of time, the four riders flanking Victoriano jerked their horses to a halt, wheeling them around to ride to the spot where their fallen leader lay.

"You got him!" Melissa shouted, holding her panting horse on a tight rein behind Slocum.

For some time the four Mexicans seemed uncertain what to do next, talking among themselves. Slocum and Melissa waited on badly winded mounts, watching the *pistoleros* talk things over in the middle of the road. Then one man dismounted, walking over to Valdez, peering down at him. Another gunman turned to stare at Slocum and the girl as another conference was held.

It was several minutes before one Mexican trotted his horse out in the brush to collect Victoriano's dun. The four men loaded Valdez's body on his horse, stretching him over the seat of his saddle.

"Now we'll know whether they aim to ride off or

fight," he told Melissa quietly, intent upon the scene in front of them.

An answer came when one rider led the dun bearing Valdez's body off the road, angling southwest, avoiding passing close to Slocum and the girl.

"They're going away," Melissa said, watching the Mexicans ride a wide circle around them through the mesquites.

"I reckon that means we'll have an easy ride the rest of the way to the Rio Grande," Slocum observed. "But just to be on the safe side, let's get moving. I don't aim to rest easy until we set foot on Texas soil."

They rode through Nuevo Laredo an hour before noon, presenting a sorry sight, a man and a woman covered with caliche dust on two badly drawn geldings. But when they came to the Rio Grande, to the shallow crossing into Texas, the girl edged her horse over to Slocum and threw her arms around his neck. She kissed him on the cheek.

"Take it easy, pretty lady," he said. "We don't want folks to get the wrong idea."

"I don't care what ideas they have, John," she said, beaming, as their horses entered the river shallows. "I owe you a debt I can never repay. Let folks think whatever they want."

They made the river crossing and trotted their mounts to the front of the city marshal's office. Slocum swung down from the saddle on wooden legs, unable to recall when he'd been so tired.

When they entered Tom Spence's office, the lawman looked up from a stack of papers on his desk. His leathery face broke into a grin. "I'll be damned," he said, coming to his feet the minute he saw Melissa. "I'll send someone out to the ranch right away to tell your father." He looked at Slocum. "You got it done, Johnny boy, only you'll need to explain that wire from Saltillo and why you didn't need the ten thousand in gold at Las Minas.''

''It's a long-winded story,'' he said, settling into a chair beside Tom's desk. ''Right now, I'm too tired to tell it to you without falling asleep. We haven't had any shut-eye in several days.''

''You can tell me later,'' Tom agreed, embracing Melissa as if she were his own daughter. ''Howard is gonna have a fit. He's so worried he ain't been able to sleep.''

''I'm okay, thanks to John,'' she replied, giving Slocum looks from the corner of her eye. ''I'll ride out to the ranch myself, if it's all the same to everyone else. I've sure been missing that place. It'll be good to be home again.''

Slocum nodded, hardly able to move from his chair. ''I'll see you tomorrow. Tell your father he owes three of Valdez's men a payday—Pedro and his friends, the ones who helped us escape.''

''He'll be generous,'' Melissa promised. She came over to the chair and bent down to kiss him, only this time, she planted wet lips on his mouth. ''Thank you, John, for risking your life to get me out of there. When I tell dad everything you did, he'll be generous with you, too.''

She whirled for the door and trotted out, mounting Tom's big roan for her ride to the ranch.

Tom was grinning at Slocum when she rode away from the rail in front of his office. ''She ain't jokin' about the fact that her dad will be generous. He'll pay you well for gettin' her back to him. To tell the honest truth, I was worried I'd never see you again.''

''Things worked out,'' Slocum remarked. ''I had to shoot four of 'em, including Victoriano himself.''

Tom's expression flattened. ''Mexico will be a better place for it. I'm sure you did what you had to do.''

''Three of Victoriano's men will be riding into town in

a few days. Anderson owes them. They got me out of Nava and gave us a couple of good horses and some guns. Without their help, I'd be in a jail cell down there. One's named Pedro Morales. The others are José and Doroteo. Make sure they get what's coming to them. Right now, I'm gonna get myself a good hotel room and sleep for a day or two. Maybe buy myself a jug of good whiskey to boot. I'm damn near too tired to sit in this chair.''

Tom shook his head. "I knew you could do it all along, John Slocum. Wasn't hardly any doubt in my mind.''

"I had plenty of doubts, Tom," he said, slumped in his chair like his spine wouldn't hold him up.

"By the way," Tom continued, "that schoolmarm by the name of Dora Fitzgerald has been askin' about you. She said to tell you that as soon as you got back from your business down in Mexico to pay her a call.'' He grinned again. "She's sure as hell a pretty thing. I'd call her the marryin' kind.''

Slocum chuckled. "For some men, Tom, there's no such thing as the marrying kind. But I'll drop by the boardinghouse to see her as soon as I've had some sleep and a bath, maybe a shave and some clean clothes. Dora's mighty pretty, but I never was one to think about settling down.''

"Maybe that'll change as you git older, Johnny boy. But in the meantime, there ain't much wrong with havin' your pick of the ladies.''

"I've had my share," Slocum agreed, remembering Anna and her sister, Annabella, from his visit to Mexico. He pushed himself up from the chair. "Right now, a little sleep and some whiskey are about all I can stand. See you tomorrow, Tom. And don't forget to see that those three Mexican boys get what's coming to them if they show up.''

Tom gave him a knowing look. "Git some rest. Tomorrow you an' me are gonna talk about what happened down yonder. I can't hardly wait to hear it.''

Slocum trudged to the office door and let himself out, after taking a long look in the direction of the Rio Grande. He'd come about as close as any man could to losing his life below that big river and, for now, he wanted to forget about it.

A special offer for people who enjoy reading the best Westerns published today.

WESTERNS!

NO OBLIGATION

Mail the coupon below

To start your subscription and receive 2 FREE WESTERNS, fill out the coupon below and mail it today. We'll send your first shipment which includes 2 FREE BOOKS as soon as we receive it.

Mail To: **True Value Home Subscription Services, Inc. P.O. Box 5235
120 Brighton Road, Clifton, New Jersey 07015-5235**

YES! I want to start reviewing the very best Westerns being published today. Send me my first shipment of 6 Westerns for me to preview FREE for 10 days. If I decide to keep them, I'll pay for just 4 of the books at the low subscriber price of $2.75 each; a total $11.00 (a $21.00 value). Then each month I'll receive the 6 newest and best Westerns to preview Free for 10 days. If I'm not satisfied I may return them within 10 days and owe nothing. Otherwise I'll be billed at the special low subscriber rate of $2.75 each; a total of $16.50 (at least a $21.00 value) and save $4.50 off the publishers price. There are never any shipping, handling or other hidden charges. I understand I am under no obligation to purchase any number of books and I can cancel my subscription at any time, no questions asked. In any case the 2 FREE books are mine to keep.

Name _____

Street Address _____ Apt. No. _____

City _____ State _____ Zip Code _____

Telephone _____

Signature _____
(if under 18 parent or guardian must sign)

Terms and prices subject to change. Orders subject
to acceptance by True Value Home Subscription
Services, Inc.

11860-5